CLEMENTINOS

CLEMENTINOS

VOICES FROM THE
CLEMENTE WRITING PROJECT

EDITED BY
MASS HUMANITIES CLEMENTE COURSE

Mass Humanities
in association with University of Massachusetts Press
Amherst and Boston

Copyright © 2024 by Mass Humanities
All rights reserved
Printed in the United States of America
ISBN 978-1-62534-809-8(paper)
Designed by Jen Jackowitz Design
Set in Crimson Text
Printed and bound by Books International, Inc.
Cover design by Sally Nichols
Cover art by Jess Rivera, *Untitled*, 2023. Courtesy of the artist.

Library of Congress Cataloging-in-Publication Data
A catalog record for this book is available from Library of Congress.

British Library Cataloguing-in-Publication Data
A catalog record for this book is available from the British Library.

Distributed for Mass Humanities by University of Massachusetts Press

CONTENTS

FOREWORD

REMEMBERING ROBERTO'S JOURNEY AND OUR OWN

I would never have done what I did in baseball without the love of the fans and the love of the Puerto Rican people. Without that I would never have done what I did.

—Roberto Clemente, 1972

When Earl Shorris envisioned a humanities program for disenfranchised people, he did not conceive it as a ballroom gala for the noblesse oblige to "help the poor," nor did he expect to create an intellectual or educational version of social work to fix broken people. In fact, he realized that traditional programs to address poverty routinely failed because they originated in wealthy peoples' misconception that poor people *needed their help* to begin with. Shorris wondered if perhaps the problem for disenfranchised men and women derived from the ways mainstream society marginalized them economically, politically, and socially in the first place. So he began a journey to meet and discuss the problems of poverty with poor people themselves—not the professionals or "experts" who spent their time studying them, analyzing them, and designing policies to regulate them.

Shorris spent years traveling around the United States, "listening to the poor." He wondered if the distinction between *force* and *power* ("force" representing the oppressive drive of humanity's dark side and "power" being the liberating and "noble instinct" of the human heart) might work in practice as it did in theory. If so, Shorris asked, "What else might be learned about poverty from the poor themselves." He continued, "If they were not understood as cases to be managed, if one could sit at the feet of the poor, and listen; if one could be a student in the school of their lives, of what had befallen them, was there not something more to be learned?"[1]

In the end, Shorris came to believe that poor people could not only "lift themselves" out of poverty if provided an opportunity, but they could be their own advocates for policy development, program design, and even reimagining democracy itself. Poor people only needed the spaces and places to develop the voice and tools to accomplish these goals. This theoretical position, steeped in real conversations with poor people, gave rise to a project offering free humanities courses to people Shorris found yearning for relevant and meaningful knowledge. He named it for the place it began, lower Manhattan's Roberto Clemente Family Guidance Center.

The Clemente Program in the Humanities has become just such a space and place for low-income people to engage in critical learning. Now operating in almost three dozen locations in thirteen states, as well as in Canada and Australia, Clemente courses reach over one thousand students every year. And, while the course began focused on bringing humanities classes to people who had no access to higher education in their communities, the programs have evolved in various ways—an evolution I imagine Earl Shorris would approve. While many sites still offer the basic Clemente course—five humanities classes in art history, philosophy, literature, American history, and writing—some programs feature support for graduates to continue with their education, earning more than the six free college credits the original course provides. Some locations now emphasize work within prisons, while others are focused on the ever-growing veteran population. Educational services have also increased, providing everything from English as a second language to financial literacy courses. As programs build deeper and wider partnerships around their communities, faculty, staff, and students demand greater opportunities to exercise not only the knowledge, confidence, and capacity they have gained but the "autonomy" that Shorris believed to be at the heart of a humanities education. Inevitably, students continue to be the driving force for Clemente programs as they develop and expand around the globe.

In Massachusetts, this dynamic took shape as students requested faculty and program coordinators to investigate ways that they might continue working on writings they had begun in class and find some way to publish

---

[1] Earl Shorris, Riches for the Poor (New York: W.W. Norton & Co., 2000), 21.

them for public consumption. Like all good artists and intellectuals, Clemente students wanted to engage the world in their conversations and imaginations. The staff at Mass Humanities (Clemente's coordinating sponsor throughout the state) garnered support from the University of Massachusetts Press and—in perhaps their only misstep—asked me to develop a curriculum and teach a class that gave students an opportunity to meet with professional writers and workshop their own pieces. *Clementinos: Voices from the Clemente Writing Project* is the result.

> Our Flowers did not hibernate in unmarked graves for seasons at a time.
>
> —Katia D. Ulysse, *Drifting*

Twelve Clemente students and I spent many weeks over the summer of '23 free writing and peer workshopping. We talked about inspiration and fears and whose voices sometimes celebrate and sometimes haunt our efforts when we put proverbial pen to paper. We were honored to talk to three award-winning authors from various genres and backgrounds who visited with us. Lester Spence, a political scientist from Johns Hopkins University and a powerful popular essayist, talked about developing as a critical thinker who still finds amazement in his work as a social scientist. His essays integrate creative storytelling with a scientific lens, linking the personal and political—or as C. Wright Mills called it, a sociological imagination. Martín Espada, winner of the Ruth Lilly Poetry Prize for lifetime achievement, also spoke of his growth as a young person engulfed in the power of words and surrounded by the rich experiences of New York City politics and Puerto Rican culture. A lawyer turned poet, Espada encouraged Clemente writers to see the world around them and the world inside them as their artistic canvas upon which to tell their truths. We were also graced by Katia D. Ulysse, Pushcart Prize nominee, whose short stories and memoirs lit up our students' curiosities. She spent over an hour answering students' questions about finding and maintaining their personal voice and focus while dealing with insecurities and fears about speaking truth to power—and to themselves.

As you examine *Clementinos*, these discussions with established writers will be clear throughout. We read Spence's "White Space, Black Space" and his personal experience selecting "Black Spaces" where he feels "at home" and "can breathe," over "White Spaces" where he is perceived as "a threat," "a statistic," "an outsider," or "an anomaly." Echoing what Du Bois first called a "sense of twoness" or "double consciousness," Clemente student Jesse Chuks describes in "Culture Shock" that same deep emotional experience of being "othered."

> While your eyeballs are fixated on mine,
> In a stare not out of affection,
> But boring deep into my weary soul,
> Mine dashed back and forth—
> East to west—looking to avoid yours.
> Hiding, not out of shame or guilt,
> But from a place of total disconnection

What we now refer to as microaggression comes to painful life as Chuks infers the emotional geography of going from "East to west" to avoid the violence of the white gaze.

Or read Alexandra Rosa's "I Am My Hair" to understand the opposite sense of joy and pride when one can not only "let down one's hair" but also find joy in a space where an ethnic identity is honored and embraced:

> Her hair shines under the light like glitter on a disco ball
> shooting dance waves through her body.
> Look at those hips go!
>
> [...]
>
> It's her hair!
> A gift from the heavens above,
> It's what makes her who she is—
> Unapologetic!
> Gracefully an Afro Latina,
> She shouts with pride!
> "I am my hair and my hair is She."

In the club, on the floor, the power of artistry and expression is released, and we can all feel the dance waves go through our bodies. All that heaven will allow—salsa and merengue, pop and lock, truth and beauty—all we know on earth and all we need to know.

Espada shared his poems and the ways in which his family's politics and culture—music and language as well as memory and imagination—filled his vision of justice and his experience of love. In "Vivas to Those Who Have

Failed: The Paterson Silk Strike, 1913," Espada heralds the vital legacy of those who struggled for liberation and passed on legacies of courage and devotion to subsequent generations.

> Strikers without shoes lose strikes. Twenty years after the weavers
> and dyers' helpers returned hollow-eyed to the loom and the steam, Mazziotti
> led the other silk mill workers marching down the avenue
> in Paterson, singing the old union songs for five cents more an hour.
> Once again the nightsticks cracked cheekbones like teacups.
> Mazziotti pressed both hands to his head, squeezing red ribbons
> from his scalp. There would be no Buffalo nickel for an hour's work
> at the mill, for the silk of bow ties and scarves. Skull remembered wood.
>
> The brain thrown against the wall of the skull remembered too:
> the Sons of Italy, the Workmen's Circle, Local 152, Industrial
> Workers of the World, one-eyed Big Bill and Flynn the Rebel Girl
> speaking in tongues to thousands the prophecy of an eight-hour day.
> Mazziotti's son would become a doctor, his daughter a poet.
> Vivas to those who have failed: for they become the river.[2]

Here in *Clementinos*, you will read about such rivers as they wind through the mountains and feed the foliage of Las Matas de Farfan. In Gris Saex's "Among Mountains," she recalls with pride her birthplace and its role as a site for resistance against colonialism and oppression.

> This Cacicazgo was well-known
> for the great battles they fought against the European oppressors. Caonabo was
> considered the lord of the Sierra (mountains) from where he fought along
>   Anacaona
> and other brave taino men and women to liberate its people. In addition, I
> learned about Las Matas to being stage for many battles that were fought
>   through its
> history, . . . where many brave women and men's blood was spilled. . . .
> I was a toddler when the Matanza de Palma Sola occurred; however, it is a
>   story that
> is told over and over among generations of Materos. It happened as the leader of

---

[2] Martin Espada, "Vivas to Those Who Have Failed: The Patterson Silk Strike, 1913, " in Vivas to Those Who Have Failed: Poems, (New York: W.W. Norton & Co., 2016), 3.

Espiritista movement, Olivorio Mateo, was assassinated, and his followers
    gathered
nearby in Palma Sola for days and were attacked by the national police as
    they refused
to leave the gathering. There is no one Matero who has not been taught
    about it. . . .
So these are some of the stories I have in my memory and part of why I love
    Las Matas
De Farfan. I prefer to call it just Las Matas, because Las Matas did/do not
    belong to
Farfan, it belongs to all who call themselves Materos and mother earth.

Farfan had been sent by the Spanish governor to steal cattle for the crown.
As Saex recalls the stories of resistance and struggle, she drops Farfan from
her identity, declaring her people—las Materos—not colonial subjects of the
crown, but the bushes and trees of the earth, who resist the corruption and
oppression of men. Saex's natural legacy is an eternal struggle for freedom.

Throughout *Clementinos*, authors claim language as crucial for their resilience and struggle. Maria M. Wilson-Sepulveda expresses the power of bilin-
gual reflection and naming as she chronicles her growth as a first-generation
immigrant woman navigating the rough terrain of poverty, prejudice,
domestic conflict, and a world that would ignore and try to silence her. She
writes:

The voice of regret, abuse, as I listened to the misguided inner voice. Deje de
    escuchar mi voz.

The voice of a new love, new life, new beginning, new goals and challenges.
Escucho la voz de mi nuevo y último amor.

The voice of my tears, mourning the loss of my parents.
Las voces de mi padres se fueron tan joven.

The voices of my baby girls and their first cries. Of them growing, meeting
    challenges, accomplishments and the voice of their future. La voz de un mejor
    futuro.

The voice of an older, many battles survived, lessons learned wiser version of me,
Whose voice will not be contained, will be expressed. Whether or not you want
    to listen to it.

Mi voz no le da ni frío, ni calor.

I write from the voices; this is my voice. Escribo de las voces. Esta es mi voz

Similarly, Louise Burrell presents her family story of resistance as they escaped the violence and segregation of Sunflower, Mississippi, and the Jim Crow South. Sunflower was "the home of Parchman State Prison, where the Freedom Riders were jailed." She continues:

> The barn where Emmett Till was killed was also in Sunflower County. My parents never talked to me about Emmett Till, but I'm sure that's why they never let me or my siblings go south to visit grandparents. Even though they had been brought up in a place that tried to teach them they were worthless, members of my family proudly marched with Martin Luther King. And I think the same strength that allowed them to march allowed my mother and father to move our family north—get jobs, join organizations, establish a foundation, and help their family and neighbors build better lives.

Resilience and resistance come not only from the legacy of families' struggles but also from the shear will and vision of women despite the patriarchal ignorance and violence of male "heads of households." Our program's final guest, Katia D. Ulysse, in her acclaimed novel, *Drifting*, explained how the narrator's mother, Manman, refused to break up the family or suffer the indignity of her husband's infidelity and his disregard for their daughters. Ulysse writes: "Manman soon found a solution to Frisner's [her husband] problem (the high cost of raising a family) and hers (the click-clicking of the prostitutes' heels on the pavement below our window). She took a factory job working from sundown to sunup. She would silence the ladies' heels as well as Frisner's please to toss her girls back to the island like unwanted catch to the sea."[3] Ulysse gives us a matriarchal hero who, faced with the myriad challenges of life in a new country, a new culture, with a new set of challenges, refuses to defer to her husband's selfishness and vanity. Her independence and will leave him walking "around the apartment like a boy who could not find his favorite toy. Manman had traded him in for a job and was punching a clock at the exact moment they were supposed to slip into bed together."

In *Clementinos*, Carman Belen finds her strength in the commitment she makes to her younger sister. Her story, "Glory," begins with her own

---

[3] Katia D. Ulysse, (New York: Akashic Books, 2014), 251.

traumatic early childhood with drug-addicted parents and abusive half-brothers. She writes:

> I was the little girl who slipped through the cracks. The girl who was neglected, physically and emotionally abused by her parents. The girl who was being sexually abused as far back as she could remember by one of her half-brothers, who would eventually be raped by him and his friends. I was the girl who never told because no one would listen. I was the girl who chose to be sexually assaulted to spare her baby sister from the same fate. I was the little girl who watched her father dehumanize his two wives, and then all three of them be too high on cocaine and drunk on blackberry brandy to realize that I was watching from the shadows. No one ever knew, because I never told. To this day, I can still smell the blackberry brandy.

The reader might be appropriately devastated by such a story, but the author found the fortitude, the foundation, and eventually a voice to persist. With the birth of her younger sister, named Glory, Belen finds a purpose, and, in the responsibility of being her sister's keeper, she finds the power to survive and rise.

> I became my little sister's main caregiver. Me, a ten-year-old girl, who didn't get a chance to ever be a child, I raised Glory, a curious four-year-old. I ensured she never had to give up her innocence or childhood. I kept her spunky, wild, and free personality intact. I made sure she was always happy. . . . As I grew from a child into a teen and then a young mother, I always had my baby sister, my best friend, to support me in ways no one on this Earth had ever done before. Many nights I cried myself to sleep, and many days I fantasized about a world where I didn't exist. I wrote suicide notes and contemplated ending my life. I felt pain and trauma from a life no one should ever experience. But the one thing, the one person that kept me alive was her. Because of her, I knew I had to be a role model. I had to make sure we had a better life as adults than we ever did as children. I had to sacrifice and work so she better life as adults than we ever did as children. I had to sacrifice and work hard so she would want to.

Belen's triumph rises with every breath she takes, each moment she chooses to persist and create. Every affirmation promises the possibility of something better, and the power of her noblest instinct resists the force of her darkest past. And she paves the way for Glory.

Does learning history prevent people, or nations, from making the same unethical and immoral decisions today? Sometimes it does, sometimes it doesn't. But whether or not we choose to use what we learn about the past to inform how we approach making our society and the world more humane and equitable is on us. As the late great poet June Jordan once said, "We are the ones we are waiting for."

—Ousmane Power-Greene

Dr. Power-Greene is an award-winning scholar, author, and educator. Above is the conclusion of the piece he shares with us in *Clementinos*, a story that comes from his long-time connection as an instructor with the Clemente program. Power-Greene reminds us of the important role that historical knowledge and memory play in the process of social change. So many of the Clemente writers in this collection—such as Saex and Burrell—have found this same power for resilience and resistance from traditions of struggle. These stories suggest Shorris got the theory and practice of Clemente right— the humanities may play a key role in the triumph and transcendence of poor people as their developing power overcomes the forces of economic, political, and social oppression.

Over the course of my own participation in the Clemente program— three years in Worcester in the early 2000s and now almost a decade in the Brockton Program—I have come to a slightly different conclusion, though. While the humanities may have intrinsic value for all people grappling with various aspects of economic violence, social marginalization, political disenfranchisement, and the myriad forms of trauma that result, I believe that "the humanities" may need Clemente students as much, if not more, than the students need the humanities. If the humanities offer each generation the intellectual, artistic, and ethical tools to investigate the human condition, then such a stockpile requires a constant rearming and revised arsenal to inform new struggles.

In her brilliant novel *Ceremony*, Leslie Marmon Silko tells us that Native Americans' ability to survive generations of attempted genocide and destruction depended heavily on their healing rituals. Ceremonies restored the present's connection to the past and empowered modern-day oppressed people with the memory of past ancestors and cultures to help them transcend trauma, carry on their struggles, and envision their futures. But the most powerful of Silko's medicine men (Descheeny) realized that healing rituals must adapt to the ever-changing forces of oppression and violence. This meant that even women like the character Night Swan must learn and inform future struggles as they create new ceremonies.

> He reasoned that because it [evil] was set loose by witchery of all the world, and brought to them by the whites, the ceremony against it must be the same. When she came, she didn't fool him for long. She had come for his ceremonies, for the chants and the stories they grew from.
>
> "This is the only way," she told him. "It cannot be done alone. We must have power from everywhere. Even the power we can get from the whites."
>
> It will take a long long time and many more stories like this one before they are laid low.[4]

For the humanities to remain vibrant and affirming they must be informed by the experiences and imaginations and the voices of Clementinos.

The complexities of our new stories of resistance and healing break through the pages of this book in so many poems and personal essays. But none may be as insightful in depicting the paralyzing moments of self-doubt that inevitably accompany the explosive moments of awakening than Judy Gustafson's ironically titled *Voiceless*. As she chronicles a day in the life of being homeless, her intellectual ability to recognize the structural forces of poverty can't always adequately squelch her internalized and moralized sense of inferiority and self-blame:

> It's bizarre, it doesn't make sense, but some irrational part of me seems to believe that if I'd tried harder or done things better, I wouldn't have gotten sick, I would have been able to succeed at one of the twenty jobs I tried on my downward slide. It's what I feel on a visceral level; logic and experience have had absolutely zero impact thus far. I am a passionate advocate for others. I fight, I rail against racism, sexism, ageism, ableism, and more. But somewhere in the depths of my soul, when I think about my own situation only, I'm classist. When I stop to think about myself, a quiet voice inside of me repeats relentlessly, "I don't belong here, I don't deserve this, it's not fair. I had a home, I went to college, I didn't do anything to deserve this, IT'S NOT FAIR." If I think professionally about those statements, I can easily acknowledge that no one deserves to be here, no one belongs here, none of this is fair for anyone. I teach

---

[4] Leslie Marmon Solko, Ceremony, (New York: Penguin Books, 1986), 126.

and believe that most Americans are a paycheck or two away from joining me, irrespective of income. But I know where I came from, and there's a little tiny piece of me always screaming in pain. So, I try to think as little as possible about my current life unless I'm actively working on changing it.

Gustafson wrestles with her own classism that forces her soul into a capitalist morality play about robust individualism, earned success, and the undeserving poor. She knows better, but she feels it all the same. By the end, however, we learn that her ritual healing occurs in the ability to work with others who are homeless, protecting those who are more vulnerable, and promoting a different set of values that truly worship the humanity of us all.

And such is the power of *Clementinos* to reinvigorate the humanities and provide new stories of inspiration and what Robin D. G. Kelley calls "Freedom Dreams." Kelley reminds us that social movements generate new knowledge and do what "great poetry always does: transport us to another place, compel us to relive horrors and, more importantly, enable us to imagine a new society."[5] Like a powerful social movement, the pages of the book speak truth to power, offering an elixir for tortured souls and inspiration to envision a better day. Let us all partake in this ceremony of healing, celebration of survival, and dedication to the future of a new humanities.

Corey Dolgon, Professor of Sociology, Stonehill College

---

[5] Robin D. G. Kelley. Freedom Dreams: The Black Radical Imagination, (Boston: Beacon Press, 2022), 61.

CLEMENTINOS

POETRY

AMONG MOUNTAINS

Gri Martinez Saex

Las Matas de Farfan/The Trees of Farfan

Among mountains, valleys, and the Macacias River there is a small town twenty-one miles
from the Haitian border, and 137 miles from Santo Domingo.
Las Matas de Farfan, is part of the San Juan Province deep into the Furnia de
Catanamatias and surrounded by the Cordillera Central Mountain Range
that runs through the heart of Quisqueya, la bella, and the Caribbean islands.
This fertile piece of land Las Matas de Farfan is where I am from.
Materos is what we are. Materos smell like history and exude pride for their town.

I heard stories as a child about our town and how we came to be and be named.
One story goes like this. Bartolome Farfan was sent to the area around 1770s to
"secure" the cattle and livestock by/for the Spanish crown. He found himself going by
the same path during his missions and this particular place provided him with a
peaceful arboleda/canopee of tamarind trees with the Macacias nearby to
rest. This resting path was then referred to as Las Matas de Farfan by passersby and
was declared the town's name by the Spanish governor.
This path was one that many others would have to take to reach what became
part of the border between Haiti and the Dominican Republic.
As a child I felt proud that my street was named Bartolome Farfan like the town
everyone was so in love with. I would roam around the streets playing hide and seek.
Going to the Damian David Ortiz School up the big hill with my teacher and my
friends was a pleasurable routine. Staying outside to look at the stars and getting
up to walk to the park only a few blocks away while smelling and tasting the sweet
nectar of flowers of Los Lorenzo's bushes was my secret. La Independencia,
Santa Lucia, La Estrelleta were streets I crossed often to get to the farmers
market, the movie theater, and my friends' homes. The weekend walks up and down
La Independencia holding my friend Nene's hand and dancing to a marching band at
Sunday concerts at the park across from the Santa Lucia Church were my favorite
pastimes.
Go forward to the beginning of fifth grade and I discovered another story of Las Matas
de Farfan. I learned what became of Bartolome Farfan's peaceful resting place,
while he was stealing, and taking possession of the land, the livestock, and the
enslaved African and indigenous people of the area that was part of the Cacicazgo de
Managua governed by Caonabo (Taino chief). This Cacicazgo was well-known
for the great battles they fought against the European oppressors. Caonabo was
considered the lord of the Sierra (mountains) from where he fought along Anacaona
and other brave Taino men and women to liberate its people. In addition, I
learned about Las Matas being the stage for many battles that were fought through its
history, such as the batalla de cachiman, la batalla de la estrelleta, Santome, March
19, etc., where many brave women and men's blood was spilled. Las Matas also
became known throughout the island for its struggles for freedom of religion as well.
I was a toddler when the Matanza de Palma Sola occurred; however, it is a story that
is told over and over among generations of Materos. It happened as the leader of
Espiritista movement, Olivorio Mateo, was assassinated, and his followers gathered
nearby in Palma Sola for days and were attacked by the national police as they refused
to leave the gathering. There is no one Matero who has not been taught about it.

My family was very involved in religious practices and because of our African, Taino, and other European roots, we practice Catholicism mixed with spiritism, etc.
Many family members were known as brujos. I spent many days of my childhood exploring los baile de palos tailing mi tia Teolinda. I loved when the borders were open during the rituals and celebrations of the Gaga.
So these are some of the stories I have in my memory and part of why I love Las Matas de Farfan. I prefer to call it just Las Matas, because Las Matas did/do not belong to Farfan; it belongs to all who call themselves Materos and mother earth.

I AM MY HAIR

Alexandra Rosa

Fierce is she?
Indeed she is.
Her curls wrap around her head like
a bouquet of wildflowers on a beautiful summer day.
She has bounce with every step she takes,
it's no mistake who's boss.
The scent of raw coconut and mango turns every head in the room,
filling the air with a tropical storm.

Her hair shines under the light like glitter on a disco ball,
shooting dance waves through her body.
Look at those hips go!

So radiant from the nappy roots to the tip of her Afro.
So bold for being big and beautiful.
Fearless is she of the controversy she may cause.

It's her hair!
A gift from the heavens above,
It's what makes her who she is—
Unapologetic!
Gracefully an Afro Latina,
She shouts with pride!
"I am my hair and my hair is She."

RED STATE (OF MIND)

Kelly Russell

When my much younger sister, in her midtwenties now,
Tells me during our biweekly zoom sesh that
She wants to move to Texas,
A few months after *Roe*'s repeal,
I laugh out loud.
Literally.
Inside, my heart pounds and I see red.
I didn't think it could get worse than it already was.
Maybe I was wrong.

Let me backtrack a little.
This isn't our first rodeo with moving.
Originally from Boston, she is calling from Flori-Duh or DeSantis-Land as I
Unaffectionately call it
When she first let it slip that she was moving to Miami two years ago
My heart dropped
For different reasons then, of course.

She tells me that Austin is calling her name,
The city,
Not the boy she was seeing.
What calls her to another red state, I don't know
My heart beats so fast in my chest, it rattles my soul.
Immediately I tell her, "You can't move to Gilead,
You are just the right age for taking."

My mind races,
thinking of dystopian books,
too-close-to-home TV shows,
and recent legal changes in the country we call home (Land of the Free, sort of).

In my worst nightmare come true,
I envision Greg Abbott and Ted Cruz's photo,
On the wall in her ob-gyn's office.
Marsha Blackburn may have been an architect, but she'll get no credit.
In Gilead (Ozona, TX; Jasper, FL; Wilcox County, AL; Anywhere, MS)
Red cloaks line a long closet,
The only prescription available to her, no matter what ails her on arrival.
Accessing Mayday or the Auntie Network is not so easy.

She is white but she is not rich.
She has red hair but emerald won't be the color of her clothing in Gilead.
There will be no crossing of state lines for birth control or family planning.
Shhhhhhhhhh
In Texas you can't even mention abortion or preventing pregnancy. It can be a
      $10,000 mistake.

I only say some of these things out loud.
I am too horrified by the possibilities.
She can see it on my face.
Nervously she laughs a little, too.
"Oh shit," she says. "I never thought of that."
"No shit," I say. "That's what you have me for."

I wonder then if I should tell her,
Once upon a time our mother was a freedom fighter
Let me go back even further . . .
In my forties now, I was nineteen when she was born.
Our age gap means she had a different version of our mother than I did.
In my lifetime, our mother was a freedom fighter.
I don't usually talk about our mother, for good reason.
That's another story, but for this,
I'll make an exception.
I've been about that *Roe* life for a long time,
Pretty much my whole life

Long before I even knew what *Roe v. Wade* was.
See, our Mama was a Rolling Stone
Just kidding!!

Our mother was a nurse in a women's health clinic.
Now I know what you're all thinking . . .
Abortion clinic and you'd be right (sort of).
There was so much more to it,
They did so much more than that, but Saturday was Abortion Day.
Saturday was the worst day.
A baptism of sorts . . .
I've been dipped in blood and body parts since I was six years old.

I went to work with our mother on Saturdays.
We could always see the protestors from a distance as we arrived,
Sometimes close to one hundred people from both sides
With their posters and megaphones.
My hand in hers, we'd run a gauntlet of opposing views:
One side full of obscene photos, broken baby dolls covered in red paint, and
venomous assumptions and insults.
The other side, full of crusaders, loudly and proudly defending a woman's right to
choose and our right to be there.
Funny, in retrospect, they all always assumed my mother to be the patient
And never a facilitator of freedom.
Once inside I would settle in an office with my backpack of treasures while our
Mother ran the recovery room.
She cared for and comforted countless women in that large quiet room filled with
Beds and reclining seats.

Fast forward a little.
I am fifteen and at home in 1994.
Our mother is at work at the clinic when a deranged man walks into a Planned
Parenthood two miles away from her clinic and starts shooting.
He goes on to a second location and starts shooting again.
It is breaking news.
When he is done, two people are dead. Five wounded.
Blood and broken glass on the pavement
The phone at my mother's clinic rings and rings.

My heart stops until I hear her voice.
It was not her clinic.

Now I'll be honest, I didn't realize she was a freedom fighter then,
but I know it now.
My sister doesn't know this at all.

So, when my much younger sister, in her midtwenties now,
tells me she wants to move to Texas
in our biweeklyish zoom sesh, I laugh out loud.
Inside, my heart pounds and I see red.
My brain aglow with the flashing of alarm lights,
Set ablaze by the screaming of sirens.
I didn't think it could get worse than it already was.
Maybe I was wrong.

Memories of another time overwhelm me.
"Got a little more time?" I ask
I grab the supplies to smoke again and seeing me, she does the same.
With the flick of a lighter, the blunt is lit, tip glowing . . .
Red.
I inhale, gather my thoughts, exhale.
And in the voice of my favorite rapper I say,
"Listen up, I got a story to tell . . ."
Then I begin.

A LETTER TO MY SON

Lynda Dolin

Jeelyn, my son, my love, my angel, no words are enough to describe the pain and bitterness that your absence causes me. This is beyond imagination and the emptiness I feel, it's inexplicable.

I still cannot believe that you're gone, I do not agree that I won't see you grow up. I refuse to live with this.

My son, my hero, how do I accept the unthinkable? I miss you so much my child! Not a day goes by that I don't think of you. Each sunrise reminds me of the hope I had seeing you alive, and each sunset makes me realize how you were suffering.

My son, my child, I miss you. My life isn't the same without you. My smile, my joy, my strength, they are all gone with you. I don't know what to do or how to move forward. Sometimes, I think I'm losing my mind. I try to smile, I pretend that I'm happy, instead of having to explain my misfortune.

My child, with you I can be honest. The truth is, I've been dying slowly since the day I learned of your illness. If I could take all this pain for you, I would have done it willingly. I was the helpless witness of your agony.

My baby boy, you weren't afraid. Every day, you were in excruciating pain, but you fought that cancer as a soldier. I prayed and begged God to let you live, but my prayers stayed unanswered.

My son, my baby, today you would have been one year old. I wanted to celebrate your birthday, I wanted to see your smile, hold your hand, sing your first Happy Birthday, help you blow out your first candle.

I repudiate the idea that I won't see you grow your first teeth. I won't see you take your first steps. I won't hear you say your first word. I won't drop you at daycare. I won't look at your first drawing. I won't see you start kindergarten. I won't take part in your karate sessions and your guitar lessons. I won't assist you in playing football with your dad. I won't buy you your first car. I won't attend your graduation ceremony. I won't see you being accepted to college. I won't meet your first girlfriend. I won't advise you on your first job interview. I won't see you flying in a plane. I won't walk with you to the aisle on your wedding day. I will never kiss my grandson, your son. You won't be present on the day of my funeral.

The only thing I witnessed was your suffering. I saw you born, I saw you fight to stay alive. After each surgery you came out stronger. I saw you smiling when I was crying. I watched you take your last breath. I attended your funeral and drove you to the grave.

My son, my love, what do I say to those fools who tell me every day that I am not the first mother to lose a child. That I must move on. I must not be dramatized. I must forget you. What do I say to them?

My son, my treasure, I hope, one day you will forgive me, because I failed to protect you from that disease. I failed to keep you healthy inside of my womb.

My son, my little baby, I would like to see you one last time, hold you in my arms, tell you how much I love you. How much I miss you, my child. You are and you will remain forever the perfect description of love for me. You were the fulfillment of all my dreams. Now, you are my only madness.

Jeelyn, my son, my love, my angel, happy birthday, and rest in peace until we meet again.

Your mom, Lynda

DEAR FRIEND

Alexandra Rosa

Dear Friend, look at you go!
It's inevitable—
Your glow,
Your spark,
Your flame that lights up the sky.

Dear Friend, so untamed and fearless
Your cape is worn with so much pride.

My Dear Friend, who dares to dream and conquer
with no fear of the future. it's clear to me who I see—
a warrior indeed.

O Dear Friend, your voice moves mountains
when you speak to the abyss
let it echo all around the world.

Dear Friend, who carries the world on your shoulders
Our turn is near, our turn is now.

Hello my Dear Friend, walking with grace and faith
the sky is never the limit so reach for the stars because
Our turn is near. Our turn is now!

I AIN'T GOT NOTHING LEFT

Christo Owens

The quilt I resonated with, "African Burial Site," but I come to it really different.
I come to it from my heart.

I ain't got nothing left.

When I saw that quilt, that's what I thought about. I ain't got nothing left.
And I know the assignment said one hundred words, but it comes to more than
one hundred words.
The ground is more than one hundred words.

See I ain't got nothing left.

I told Mommy, I said, what? What?

I ain't got nothing left.

After going through that surgery, that rehab, the memory! Them people!
Your pearls, my pearls, your opal, that blue opal, them jades! All mother's, all of
them!
Mother's quilt. Mother's quilt! She made it for me! Terry's quilt! Chucky's quilt!
Ricky's quilt, all of them, they just gone now!

I ain't got nothing left!

And Mother said—
"Child, what's wrong with you?
I said, "What! What you mean Ma? I got something left?"

And she said, "You got breath in your body and living Spirit!
Yeah, and you got hope!
You got a whole lot of hope! What they got? Nothing but the dirt, the dirt that
God made them from and now taking them back to!"

Ahh! So! There's a smile to go along with that hope!

The hope and the smile I can carry by the grace of God!

And so you can, too!

SALTY HUMAN BEES

Jessie Chuks

I am Salt, I give taste, I add flavor
I am the chief ingredient
I am the most valuable of all
I know my worth, my usefulness
The chef can't deny this
You may not notice my presence
But my absence is always loud.
I make a lasting impression
I am Salt.

I am Salt, I preserve
I am not restricted to the kitchen
I preserve freshness, I prevent rottenness
I preserve originality, I prevent decay
I preserve—ask the scientist
A little at a time, that's all you need
Moderation is the word
Just a friendly reminder, too much is too dangerous
I am Salt.

I am Salt, I destroy
But only the bad guys
I keep your gums safe from them
At the dentist's recommendation.
I could sting you like a Bee

But don't worry, it's to keep you safe
For with each sting comes healing
And a relief
I am Salt

I am Bee, I am a treasure
I provide quality food
I produce honeycomb
I pollinate and cross-pollinate seeds and nuts
I plant trees
I prevent soil erosion
I am responsible for your coffee and spices
I should be cherished
I am Bee.

I am Bee, I make honey
I make Beeswax and Bee pollen
I heal, with the numerous medicines I make
I make Bee venom and Royal Jelly
I fertilize plants—for humans
Now that Salt mentioned it
I sting, to protect me and mine
I sting to preserve life, my life
I am Bee

I am Bee
I have a colony, I sting to protect it
From Humans' chemicals and appropriation. You bet I do
I sting to protect my beehives
I sting Humans, they take everything I make for myself
Even after I travel from place to place
To transport and fertilize seeds for them
I sting humans, they always invade
I am Bee

I am Human, I guess this is the place where I speak for myself
I command, I control, I dominate to thrive
I am needy, I am selfish, I am greedy

When I discovered you, it was because I needed you
When I did some studies, actually lots of studies,
It was to maximize your benefits and your usefulness to me
I like putting everything to good use
I do not like waste, so I made sure to find numerous uses for you
I am Human

I am Human, you said I like to invade
Of course I do. What did you think? How else do I survive?
I am an opportunist, I am the selfish coordinator, the greedy nature consumer
I like to have my way, I like to be in charge
That way I become the beneficiary of your multiple benefits
I need everyone, I need the values you bring, I always need them
I may be a little self-centered, or outright selfish
But I need you to survive, I need you all to keep going
I am Human.

I am Human
Even though I am not mindful of the damages I cause you
I realize that when I invade, it affects you
I pledge to preserve like Salt, to protect like Bee
To coordinate and organize better
To appreciate and care for you and everyone
I value you, I cherish you, I treasure you
I know better, I will do better. Still—
I am Human.

DEAR POETRY

Gri Martinez Saex

Dear Poetry:
I seek your wisdom
In this moment of sorrow
Of grief
I seek the stillness
And closeness to self and others
I ask you to let me use you as a vehicle
To reconcile and mend my heart
In this healing journey of mine
The killings and deaths increment every day
Like recurrent nightmares
To our collective psyches
And I know that we shall overcome

WHAT WE SEE WITHIN

Hava Zejnullahu

Imagine strolling along a picture-perfect beautiful island beach
nothing but a gentle breeze flowing through your hair.
You amble along barefooted
for miles aside the clear turquoise water's edge.
The cool refreshing ebb and flow of the ocean
surrounds your feet as if an old friend just gave you a warm hug after a long
    journey.

You hear the faint peaceful singing
of the Elfin Woods Warblers in the distance
they fly back and forth
amongst the tall, lush tropical greenery.

You discover that even the soft, fine and deliciously velvet sand
under your feet
is comforting
stable even.

As you look out into the abyss of limitless ocean
an alluring ray of genial sunshine kisses your face
and you smile.
Smile from the secure embrace
of such an unimaginable vision
of enchanting paradise
the Lord has bestowed upon you.

So-much-so, that it truly illuminates your soul
like the baptism of a newborn child.

You can't help but close your eyes
take a deep breath in
to be engulfed by the perfect combination
of tropical flowers
coconut and suntan lotion
with just a hint of sea salt
to heighten your senses.
To experience such beauty
tranquility and calmness
is to be blessed.

I never had the opportunity
to experience such beauty
on an actual desert island
but when I am with you
I am provided with that pure at heart peace of mind.
The kind you only experience
when you are on this imaginary island.

Who would have ever thought
I would be so fortunate,
to come across such an incredible human being?

THE SOUND OF LOVE

Alexandra Rosa

A newborn crying when it's just been born.
Ssshhh, mama whispers as the baby settles down.

The laughter of a family reunion that can be heard
miles away.

Children playing in the rain, splashing and jumping
as if life had no worries at all.

Animals communicating with one another, sending the
mind straight to the jungle.

The wind that gently caresses your skin and plays with
your hair.

A saxophone player soothing the soul of a crowd;
let it tingle down your spine.

A grandmother's story about how she survived poverty
growing up.

The world around us carries sounds of the unknown.

The sound of love is everywhere, just listen closely,
embrace the moment and carry that sound in memory

Forever.

CULTURE SHOCK

Jessie Chuks

While your eyeballs are fixated on mine,
In a stare not out of affection,
But boring deep into my weary soul,
Mine dashed back and forth—
East to west—looking to avoid yours.
Hiding, not out of shame or guilt,
But from a place of total disconnection

Disconnection from love and affection
From care, understanding and friendship.
Yet deep down you still stared
Seeking for what is not hidden.
Like an archeologist digs, you dug
To unravel a mystery, layer upon layer.
You dug, while I dashed back and forth—
East to west—to avoid yours, till you let go

Nothing hidden, nothing unraveled,
Just a difference in societal norms
yours to stare, mine not to
For when we stare deep, it is to connect the one we love.
For the eye makes a connection to the soul
Both are well, and welcomed, at least in my world.
But I wish your stares came with care and with love
Devoid of judgment, meanness, unkindness

So when next we meet at the park, or elsewhere
I hope we look at each other with understanding
I truly hope we stare with the care that brings
Humanity and the connection and redemption it deserves.
For through the eyes, the hearts connect
Through the eyes, we see the soul

And access the love that lays beneath.

THE VOICES LAS VOCES

Maria M. Wilson-Sepulveda

I hear the voice of the little girl from a long time ago,
Who was happy, scared, sad and sometimes alone. Pobre niña

The voice of a new language. ¿ Dónde se fue mi language y mi voz?
The voice of living in a new country. ¿ Mi patria dónde se fue?
Insecurity overwhelmed my voice.

I hear the voice of my mother.
Her tone, her tears, her anger.
The voice of a single mother trying to make it, survive and bring us forward.
Cierro mis ojos, as tears fill my eyes and my soul. Mami quiero entender tu voz.

I hear the peaceful voice of my father.
Peaceful as he didn't have to fight to survive the struggle of raising us.
I don't hold it against you Papi, pero te perdiste mucho.

I hear the voice of my paternal grandmother. Her voice always filled with a smile.
Mama Abuela!
Versus the voice of my maternal grandmother that I cannot recall as she died too
    young.
Bendición Abuela.

I hear the voice of a young girl making her way.
I hear the voice of a teenager and her first kiss. Recuerdo ese primer beso.

The voice of a young adult, misguided, and pointed in many directions.

The voices of everyone telling me what to do, as they wanted to live their life
through me.
The many voices telling me to do the right thing, be the example for my sisters to
follow.
Hiding my voice as I needed to be what everyone else wanted me to be. Perdí mi
voz.

The voice of regret, abuse, as I listened to the misguided inner voice. Dejé de
escuchar mi voz.

The voice of a new love, new life, new beginning, new goals and challenges.
Escucho la voz de mi nuevo y último amor.

The voice of my tears, mourning the loss of my parents.
Las voces de mi padres se fueron tan joven.

The voices of my baby girls and their first cries. Of them growing, meeting
challenges, accomplishments and the voice of their future. La voz de un mejor
futuro.

The voice of an older, many battles survived, lessons learned wiser version of me.
Whose voice will not be contained, will be expressed. Whether or not you want
to listen to it.
Mi voz no le da ni frío, ni calor.

I write from the voices; this is my voice. Escribo de las voces. Esta es mi voz.

PROSE

GLORY

Carmen L. Belen

I am convinced that any suffering we endure is nothing, compared to the
glory that he will reveal to us later.

—*Romans 8:18*

I lay in my bed, the top bunk, of a wooden bunk bed. Staring at the ceiling, at
3 a.m. while everyone in our little one-bedroom apartment slept. The one-
bedroom apartment was shared between my mother, my little sister, and me.
The silence is broken by the sound of the house phone, loud rings that sound
like alarms. I lay there paralyzed. My mother, who is sleeping in the living
room, answers the phone. There was a pause, then I could finally hear her.
"What did you say?" she said, right before she hung up.

I could hear her in a soft yet rattled voice, telling the man that I now call
my stepfather "El papa de las niñas," the girls' father, she said in Spanish. I lay
there, my heart racing. The moment I felt was coming had arrived. Prior to
the phone ringing, I felt unbalanced. I felt a shift in my life. The emptiness. So
when my mother walked into our bedroom and cut the light on, I said, "Papi
died." She didn't say anything, her face went blank, and she nodded as her
eyes filled with tears. We told my sister, who at the time was only five years
old, so she didn't really comprehend it.

The days to follow were all a blur, a web of memories that blended into
each other so I wouldn't be able to say if it had been hours or days or even
weeks. Perhaps because I was only eleven years old, or just the way my brain
grieved the death of my father. I recall the drive from Massachusetts to New
Jersey. In my grandmother's station wagon, with my mother, my aunt, my

two sisters, my little cousin, and my grandmother. I remember the quaint little hotel room we all shared. I remember getting to the church and barely making it to the casket before I ran out scared. I had never seen a dead person before, and I didn't imagine the first to be my father.

I recall the morning in the cemetery. Everyone was crying as they lowered the casket to the ground. My eldest brother scooped me up and carried me out because I wanted to jump into the grave. I just lost my father; no little girl wants to lose her father. All of these days were webbed together. I couldn't tell you an exact timeline, and while all this was very traumatic, this is not my origin story. It is a small moment in the trauma of my entire childhood.

What I did not mention was that my father was addicted to cocaine. Three weeks prior to his death I said goodbye to him for the last time. My mom came to pick my sister and me up from my dad's house, at the end of summer vacation. As we were leaving my father gave me a hug and said, "I'm glad I got to see you one last time." The words always danced in my mind because even as a child they felt eerie. I knew I was never going to see my father again. I never told anyone. So when my father hung himself on September 17, 1998, just a little after midnight, I knew before the phone rang. I felt it in my stomach.

I was a little Puerto Rican girl who grew up in a home with three drug-addicted parents. Yes, three. My father, his wife, and my mother. Also in the house were my two older half-brothers and my baby sister. I was the little girl who slipped through the cracks. The girl who was neglected, physically and emotionally abused by her parents. The girl who was being sexually abused as far back as she could remember by one of her half-brothers, who would eventually be raped by him and his friends. I was the girl who never told because no one would listen. I was the girl who chose to be sexually assaulted to spare her baby sister from the same fate. I was the little girl who watched her father dehumanize his two wives, and then all three of them be too high on cocaine and drunk on blackberry brandy to realize that I was watching from the shadows. No one ever knew, because I never told. To this day, I can still smell the blackberry brandy.

While my entire childhood was traumatic, and probably someone's "villain origin story," my origin story started on February 12, 1993, when my baby sister, Glory, was born. I remember that day, I remember the room where I was sitting. Burned into my core memory. Weirdly, I was alone, in the bedroom, watching *The Bodyguard* with Whitney Houston. I was about six years old, watching the moment when Whitney is singing "I Will Always Love You" when my "other mother" walked in to tell me that my baby sister was born. The core memory of that song that till this day my sister jokes about because I cry whenever it comes on. Because "I will always love her."

Not much changed after my mother ran away from my father with my little sister and me. We ended up in Massachusetts. My mother stopped doing drugs but continued to be an alcoholic. She constantly left, leaving Glory and me home alone while she frequented bars and left for days at a time with random men. I became my little sister's main caregiver. Me, a ten-year-old girl, who didn't get a chance to ever be a child, raising Glory, a curious four-year-old. But I ensured she never had to give up her innocence or childhood. I kept her spunky, wild, and free personality intact. I made sure she was always happy. I became my sister's keeper.

The reason I am who I am today is because I had my baby sister, Glory, to get me through my darkest days and my toughest nights. Growing up in a three-parent household filled with neglect and drugs was traumatic, but locked in my bedroom I had my baby sister. Being sexually abused and knowing it was wrong, I allowed it to protect my baby sister. Grieving my father's death, when my mom would get angry that we cried because "if it was her, we wouldn't" I had my baby sister to look out for me while I cried so my mom wouldn't get mad at me. She claims I was her savior, but she was mine.

As I grew from a child into a teen and then a young mother, I always had my baby sister, my best friend, to support me in ways no one on this Earth had. Many nights I cried myself to sleep, and many days I fantasized about a world where I didn't exist. I wrote suicide notes and contemplated ending my life. I felt pain and trauma from a life no one should ever experience, but the one thing, the one person that kept me alive was her. Because of her, I knew I had to be a role model. I had to make sure we had a better life as adults than we ever did as children. I had to sacrifice and work hard so she would want to.

I got part-time jobs as soon as I could to give her the best Christmases and birthdays. I hustled to keep a roof over her head and food in her stomach. Through poverty-stricken moments in our childhoods, I found ways for her to have fun and not notice the struggles we were facing. So many times we faced homelessness, when we slept in the car and I would pretend we were on these crazy road trips, although we were parked in the back of a dark parking lot. Watching her grow from a happy carefree child to a decent adult gives me pride. Pride in knowing my sacrifices were not made in vain. Today she is a preschool teacher and an amazing role model. She is caring, loving, and ambitious. Most importantly she is my best friend.

Being able to guide her through life and protect her prepared me to become the best mother I could for my four daughters. Many people see me as a victim of unfortunate circumstances; however, I am a survivor. I knew I never wanted my children to experience what had been normal for me in my life. My children know they have an open line of communication to tell me anything and everything under the sun. I never allowed them to witness drug abuse, and I made sure the people I kept around them were safe. If there was a family member that my child expressed made them feel uncomfortable or uneasy, I simply limited contact to little or none. My village was small, to say the least. This, however, is how I work toward giving them a childhood they never have to recover from.

As for my relationship with my biological mother, she lives in Florida, and we have become estranged. Although we never had the best relationship, I tried to maintain one with her regardless; however, she refused to respect my boundaries. I heard my "other mother" suffered many health conditions, as a result of years of drug and alcohol abuse. She passed away in 2014. I hadn't had a relationship with her since my father passed away. At that time, I also discontinued my relationship with my half-brothers. I shut the door to my traumas. My sister Glory as I mentioned before is my best friend, my favorite person in the whole world. Not a day goes by that we do not talk. Oftentimes, we sit on the phone, going on about our lives, not even really talking but just knowing that we're there. When life gets to be overwhelming and I feel as though I'm lost, she's there to remind me of everything we overcame and to put me on the right path.

I spent many years negatively coping with my traumas and hiding them. After seeing how my past was affecting my life as an adult, I decided to seek counseling to help me overcome some of my childhood trauma, or at least come to terms with it. I am still a work in progress. I am a survivor who is still surviving every day. Telling my story is just one of the many steps I have taken in my recovery and growth.

THE GREATEST GIFT

Larry Madden

I

I was jolted awake. Screams, name-calling, and curses downstairs. "You'll never amount to anything." The screen door slammed, my oldest sister running across the lawn, crying, again. Mom alone in the kitchen. Best left that way. The lawn mower is running, my older brother behind it because Dad's at work. The vacuum cleaner is also running, my other sister behind it. The two "babies"? Who knows. The sheets were hot, sticky, the room stifling despite the fan on the chair at the foot of the twin beds. Time to enter the daily unknown. Home.

A Victorian; "1894" above the little attic window. The right half nestled in the shade of an ancient maple tree; the left, driveway and garage. A porch in the shade, a porch in the sun, a covered, wraparound porch in front. Three doors, three ways to get out.

I loved summers. They seemed to last forever and yet, not. We were fortunate to have lived in a small rural town on a dead-end street. Often, bikes would be strewn across the yard, across the driveway, dropped randomly by the six of us and our friends until suddenly they would be mounted and disappear to the swimming hole, the woods on the hill, the sand pit at the end of the road, or even the other side of town: the cemetery, the white clapboard library, the river below the falls to fish. The church.

It was my twelfth summer. Tremorous changes were happening. My legs and back ached. Growing pains my mother said, "and my damn grocery bill shows it." I fit differently in my bed. Bike seat needed adjusting. For years, I would fake sleeping, keeping one eye open like a new moon hoping to catch a glimpse of my older brother as he changed, fascinated by his hair and his proportions. It was happening to me, and I reveled in it.

Sometimes, I would help a friend with his paper route. Get the job done quicker so we could get back to the swimming hole sooner. I felt shielded when he was there. The older boys would hurl names at him, "sissy," "cup-cake." He never seemed to be afraid of them like I was. He found different names and threw them back in between the cannon balls off the rope swing that they landed around him. He was fifteen, like the others.

One hot afternoon, after delivering the last paper, we headed down a long hill without breaking, daredevils. Suddenly, my friend screeched to a stop.

"Hey, want to see something really beautiful?" he asked. "Come on, follow me."

We left our bikes against a tree and walked into the woods. I had never seen this piece of the woods. Within minutes, we were at a flowing stream, five feet wide, rocky, and shaded by arching trees.

"This is one of my favorite places," he told me as he reached into his shirt pocket and pulled out matches and a joint.

"Ever smoke grass before?" he chuckled.

"No, but it's okay with me. My older sister and her fiancé do." I promised to keep it a secret.

"Secrets are good." He lit the joint and handed it to me. "Just a little bit, inhale slowly, just a bit."

Coughing and laughing immediately followed. We repeated the ritual.

"So, what do you think? You alright?"

I stood transfixed, staring at the speckled, wavering light through the trees, birdsong in the hot breeze.

"Yeah, yeah . . . I'm okay. I like this."

"Good, now stop smiling so much," he roared.

Without warning, he pulled off his shirt, kicked off his flip-flops, and dropped his pants.

"Come on take yours off too, let's go in."

Wading into the knee-deep water, he pounced, caught me in a half nelson and dunked me into the water. I managed to grab both his ankles in a hug as he tried getting away, tripping him. Splashing and laughing. He stared at me. We stood there, our masculinities on full display. My eyes followed him to his knees in front of me. I squeezed my eyes as tightly as I could, trying to stop the waving, spinning of the ground. Once steadied, we laid on our backs, allowing the water to wash over us.

Jumping back on our bikes, my friend asked, "Do you want to come back tomorrow?"

"Sure," I said. "If you do. Want help with the papers again?"

"If you want to. See you tomorrow."

He rode towards his house. I pedaled towards mine.

At dinner that evening I ate as fast as I could, barely looking up. I was ashamed, delighted, and curious. I wanted to be alone. A strange sensation in my belly squeezed so hard, pushed past the lump in my throat, and trailed wet down my cheeks. I swung in the hammock under the maple tree until my thoughts were interrupted by my mother.

"Keep an eye on the boys while I do dishes with your sister. Oh, tonight you're sleeping downstairs on the couch with your brothers. It's too hot upstairs."

"Why me? Why not someone else?" Her voice irritated me. "Leave me alone."

"Don't back-talk me, I'll slap your face."

I put the boys against the wall, and I took the edge. I couldn't fall asleep for what seemed like hours. In synchrony, all of my father's clocks rang midnight. Why was the room so cold? Where was the wind coming from? I pulled the sheet over the boys and turned into the room. My heart froze, my breath vanished. In the corner, by the windows, a limpid, gray woman, scraggly hair, ancient, in a bathrobe identical to my mother's, floating, summoning me with one long bony finger. I slammed my eyes shut and waited to breathe. I cracked one eye open. She was there, laughing at me. My primal scream filled the house. When I opened my eyes, she was gone. The boys were sleeping peacefully next to me.

Later, at breakfast, Mom snipped, "You're awfully quiet. What did you do wrong?"

"Just tired. Didn't sleep well," I said, dropping my dishes in the sink, disappearing out the door.

Wake as one person, go to bed another. Hiding in plain view.

II

When I was led in, they were all sitting behind a large table, a single chair facing them: company commander, first sergeant, JAG lawyer, wife, and son.

My son screamed, "Daddy" and ran to me. I was too weak to pick him up and afraid that if I started to cry, I may not be able to stop. I had to stay strong, but I ached all over. My chest constricted to keep the feelings locked away. My abdomen squeezed tight to prevent me from soiling myself. My head spun, I wanted to scream.

"Please, this isn't me. I don't want to do this anymore."

I hugged my son briefly, tightly. Sadness, confusion, fear ran down his cheeks. My wife came and took him by the hand.

"Sergeant," my commander said, "I don't think we need to explain why all of us are here. Please stand. You are in violation of Article 86, Uniform Code of Military Justice. I have not yet made a decision as to how I will proceed. This morning, everyone here will have a chance to speak, if they wish. I will come to a decision after that."

I knew that there would be consequences, a steep price to pay. I had, after all, walked away from the army. AWOL, they call it. Mediterranean vacation and fuck you, I called it. It was short-lived, some days really, before the body odor, hunger, and empty wallet caught up with me. I had to return to base and face the music.

The MPs at the gate asked for my ID, examining me curiously.

"Please wait here for a moment, Sergeant," one spit-shined and sharply pressed MP said. Moments later the flashing lights arrived, the cuffs were placed on my wrists, and I was driven off to the station.

"Sergeant, we have specific orders to detain you until your commander can be notified. Before we search you, do you have anything to declare?"

I had already rid myself of any incriminating evidence: syringes, spoons, little white bags. I was thoroughly searched, put into a drab green jumpsuit, and placed in a cell. Metal bed, sink, and toilet for all to see. I wanted nothing more than to disappear, to never again hurt or fail anyone. I wanted to scream, swing, hit. Instead, I sat shaking on the edge of the bed, a stray dog in a kennel.

"Your commander said you're ours for the weekend. And a holiday weekend to boot," they laughed. "We're all nice guys, don't worry. Is there anything we can do for you?"

"Can you call my wife, my son, and let them know I am here?"

"She's been advised not to have any contact with you, at this time. It's a small base, she'll hear, trust me."

"Your first sergeant has contacted JAG, a lawyer has been assigned to you," the MP lieutenant informed me.

I knew it was a matter of time. Several hours had passed since last using. Lying on the hard bed, blanket over my head, the cramps came first like hands inside kneading my guts. Then the sweats and chills, runny nose. Vomiting. "Hey, what's the matter with you? You alright?" one MP asked.

"I'm okay, think I ate something bad, maybe. OH FUCK." The diarrhea, down my legs, in front of them all.

"Oh damn, you're cleaning that up yourself, soldier."

"Lieutenant, I think we need medical backup here," one MP yelled.

The doctor arrived several hours later. A quick exam, "Soldier, I'll pre-scribe something to help, but honestly, you've got a long weekend."

At the hearing, my lawyer leaned on the table and said, "Sergeant, if your commander decides to, do you understand that you may face up to one month in confinement, reduction in rank, and forfeiture of pay? You could also be given a dishonorable discharge." "Yes," I replied. The commander then opened it to the others.

"Well, I'll go first," First Sergeant drawled. "I want to see you do the right thing; get the help you need, Sergeant. The army is ready to offer you that help; twelve weeks inpatient detox, the last four of which you'll be joined by your wife for family therapy. If you refuse help, I have recommended a dishonorable discharge."

My wife spoke next. "John, I want you to get help, please. I will join you in Germany for the last month," she cried, "but I can't promise anything other than that, except I'll want a divorce if you don't go."

Drug and alcohol treatment or discharge. Drug and alcohol treatment or divorce. Failed drug and alcohol treatment and discharge and divorce. The price I had to pay was clear.

"I'm ready for help, Sir. I can't do this anymore."

I was brought to the airport by ambulance. Once there, a medical triage team sorted us; white patient identification bracelets for everyone, except me. Bright red, psych patient. The voices all around me drifted to a distant murmur. My feet wouldn't move.

"Sergeant, SERGEANT," a nurse hollered. "Please board by the front door."

Once seated, I stared out the window, pulling my left sleeve down over my bracelet, holding it tightly in place. Once in the air, a nurse approached me,

"You okay over here?" I nodded without taking my eyes from the window. Twelve weeks inpatient, three months. I made a solemn promise to myself; talk about everything, everything except my sexuality. Take it to the grave.

Once in Germany, I checked into the hospital compound's guest house. Room 310.

"Guten Morgen," my temporary roommate said, barely looking up. Six foot two, blond, marine, stretched out on one of the two twin beds, in his underwear. "I'm sorry, let me throw some clothes on, it's just that it's a bit warm in here." He extended his hand, "Alan."

"John," I muttered, staring at my shoes. I wanted desperately to run back to the desk and ask for a different room. Tug-of-war voices in my head. STOP, please STOP, I am a married man, a father. Every ounce of me wanted a drink, a fix . . . wanted to be grabbed by his hands and thrown on the bed. I unpacked in silence, being watched by big, blue eyes.

"So, what brings you here? I'm here for surgery but it's not scheduled until Friday," Alan said, trying to initiate some conversation. "Hey, I was going to grab some grub soon. Want to join me? The hospital has a great mess hall."

My words were stuck in my throat, the air I needed barely getting around them.

"Sure, I am hungry."

"So, what brings you here?" he asked again.

"I really don't want to talk right now, if that's okay?"

"Let me know when you're ready to chow down."

His chattiness saved an awkward dinner. I heard everything, absorbed nothing, and devoured my food. Back in the room, I stretched out, exhausted. He lay on his bed, reading.

"I was thinking of going for a nice walk later, if you care to join me. If not, I understand. You must be tired," he said. "You're a man of few words. There's a nice park just down the road, thought you may enjoy it."

We walked in silence interrupted only by Alan's small talk. I struggled to hold back tears. Unsuccessfully.

"Hey, let's sit here. Take a break. You okay?" he inquired, sincerely.

"I'm sorry, this has never happened to me before," I assured him.

Violently, something broke inside of me, like a dam bursting. I sat shaking and sobbing, passersby staring. Through tears and snot I told Alan everything, apologizing continuously. I told him about my family, drug use, my stint in the seminary, homelessness at eighteen, army enlistment, pregnancy after first drunk night together, marriage two months after meeting, a petrified child trying to play Daddy and raise a baby. I continued, eventual heroin use, AWOL, regretting ever having been born. Everything streamed out, unstoppable. "I think I'm a fucking queer." Without warning, I heaved my supper across the grass between us.

"Maybe we should head back," Alan said and got up and walked away. I had fucked up again.

Back in the room, a palpable silence surrounded us. I knew that in the morning, Alan would be gone. That he would escape room 310 in the middle of the night. Couldn't blame him.

The sound of running water woke me and I rolled over to see Alan standing naked at the sink shaving. "Good morning," he said in the mirror.

"Good morning," I mumbled. "I'm surprised you're still here. Thought for sure you'd have run from me."

"Why would I do that, John?" He rinsed his chiseled face, dried off, walked to his dresser, and pulled on his underwear. "Actually, just the opposite. I couldn't wait for you to wake up," he said, sitting on the edge of my bed.

"You scared me, and I really didn't know what to do or say when you shared your stuff with me. I've never seen someone cry like that before, John." A single tear fell from his eyes. "It's my turn. This is all so scary. We have the same birthday, I also am the fourth out of six in a Catholic family. John, I was in the seminary in the same damn city as you, at the same fucking time. I left and joined the marines the same time you chose army. Now, here we are in this goddamn room together. He wiped his face on his arm. "John, you are not alone. I have never told anyone, but . . . I have always questioned who I am too. I'm gay. There I said it. If you're man enough to say it, I'll say it too."

The days that followed were glorious. Long walks and talks. A run every morning. Cake and coffee every afternoon, while Randy Travis sang "Digging Up Bones." Then, treatment started, and Alan had his surgery. I frantically needed to know if he was okay, but leaving the treatment facility was prohibited. I used my sheets to climb out the window and scurried to the main building. I found him lying in bed, his left hand wrapped and elevated on pillows, a Walkman in his ears while he wrote.

"What the hell are you doing here? You're batshit crazy."

I climbed in bed beside him, "What are you writing?"

"The lyrics from 'Like a Virgin.' I was going to send them to you but, you're here now."

"Let me see."

I made it through the wilderness
Somehow, I made it through
Didn't know how lost I was until I found you
I was beat, incomplete
I'd been had, I was sad and blue, but you made me feel
Yeah, you made me feel shiny and new.

We agreed to continue meeting every afternoon for our ritual of cake and coffee. The last day before his return to the embassy, I arrived at our usual time, same table. Randy Travis was still singing but Alan wasn't there. The waitress, with her beehive bouffant hairdo, came over to the table and handed me a note. "He said to give this to you, honey. He was here about half an hour ago." I opened the note, "ROOM 310."

My feet couldn't move fast enough, up two and three steps at a time. I knocked on the door. No answer. It was unlocked. He was in the shower, and in no time at all, so was I. Dripping wet, we fell onto the bed. Alan reached over and turned the volume up on the radio. Later, lying in each other's arms, Alan said, "I have an idea. Let's write each other a letter this evening. I will say everything about how I am feeling, the best I can. Can you do the same?" I said of course I could and would. "Then tomorrow, when I leave, we'll exchange them." I agreed.

We met the next day and, as agreed, exchanged our letters, forced again to be just the uniforms we wore. He craned his head backward as the olive-green bus pulled away. Although we had promised to wait one day before opening our letters, I ripped mine open as the bus turned the corner and dropped out of sight. I felt complete and calm for the first time in years. "I will see you in Frankfurt, November 24th. I booked a room at the airport Hilton." When I got back to my room, I tucked the letter in my notebook for safekeeping.

Saturday, the twenty-fourth, our first overnight pass from the program. That morning, in our group therapy, we were all asked to explain where and with whom we were spending our pass, as well as which AA meeting we would attend. Our therapist questioned me extensively as to why Frankfurt if my wife was in Stuttgart. Strange, he said. I was lying through my teeth.

The next day, Sunday, my wife arrived at the treatment facility shortly after I had returned from Frankfurt. Awkward, uncomfortable day. I struggled to have a conversation with her. Monday morning, we gathered back in our group therapy. We all knew that if the psychiatrist joined us, and he did, someone was going on the hot seat. I leaned over to my roommate, Skip, and asked if he had any idea who it was. "We'll soon find out," he replied.

The therapist started on his left, going around the circle, asking each soldier how their pass went. When he got to me, he said nothing and skipped over to Skip. My head felt like it was imploding. All eyes were on me. When he finished the circle, he reached into his coat pocket. NO, it isn't, it can't be. It was. I had no idea that the letter from Alan had fallen out of my notebook and the therapists had it the whole time. They knew where I was going on my pass. They knew who I was meeting, and they knew why. They knew who I was. He read the letter to the whole group.

When I came to, I was on the floor between chairs, covered in vomit. The psychiatrist was fanning me while someone took my blood pressure. They helped me to the exam room. I assured them, repeatedly, that I was okay, that I had no thoughts of hurting myself. I just wanted to sleep.

The next four weeks were difficult. Coming out to my wife was painful for us both. We left dinner one evening and went for a cold, snowy walk. I noticed a newfound strength inside, an unfamiliar calmness, and I simply told her. We cried and held each other. Our future, the future of our family, instantly became a question mark. All that we knew, all that we could promise, was to be there for each other and, more than anything, to be there for our son.

The graduation ceremony was on the twenty-fourth of December, Christmas Eve. My wife and I packed our bags in the car, said our goodbyes, gave our hugs, and hit the highway to drive overnight to Italy. We wanted desperately to arrive before our son woke, get his gifts under the tree, and surprise him. The weather cooperated, the car behaved, and we pulled into our driveway at 0500.

That Christmas was "the best of times . . . the worst of times." It was my first Christmas complete, whole, and honest. Yet it was poignant realizing it was the last Christmas as a family together. A profound sadness swept over me, again and again, every time I looked at our son, beaming with joy because we were all together, too young to understand what was around the corner.

I sat sipping my hot chocolate, the fire crackled beside us, warming my little man as he played. Mom-wife-soldier was in the kitchen: roast beef, Yorkshire Pudding, and roasted potatoes like every year. I walked up behind my wife, wrapped my arms around her, and kissed her. "I am so sorry," I whispered through tears. Wiping her hands on her apron, she turned and took my hands.

"We will be okay, all of us. It may suck at times, but we will get through this. John, don't feel sorry, please. You are giving us the greatest gift you can, yourself, true, real John. He may not understand now but he will," she said tilting her head towards where our son played contently.

III

We were having our first dinner party at our new place in Montebuono. An anniversary party for my husband and me combined with a sort of house-warming. The menu: antipasto of cured meats, cheeses, and bruschetta, Rigatoni all'amatriciana, assorted grilled meats, and a salad. Dessert of course. The table was set with wine, water, and bread: like every altar at every mass.

Everyone arrived as I was outside checking on the steaks, sausages, and fresh pancetta sizzling over the coals. My husband popped open a cold first bottle of Prosecco wine, opened before the kisses were finished, a toast given, and every male jockeyed for dominance over the grill. Opinions whirling as fast as the laughs.

A refreshing breeze blew in from the mountains, the sunset, a swath of orange, pink, and purple, visible from the kitchen windows. In usual fashion, the conversations were many and loud, arms tangled across the table as food was passed. When people reached for seconds, I knew all was well. "John, you suck. You cook better than Lucia." We all laughed at the slap Antonio received for that comment. Two hours later, homemade tiramisu, brought as a gift.

The conversations, the icing on the cake. We explained where we met, what brought us to Italy in the first place, why the return in retirement. And family, the never-ending questions about family. "Tomorrow, in fact, we are planting seven trees: one for each of our grandkids," my husband added. Then, like the shock of an earthquake in the middle of the night, Valerio asked, "John, why no pictures of your son or grandson on Facebook ever? We don't know anything about your family."

I didn't know where to put myself. My husband took my hand under the table. I had no idea where to begin: my son's difficult childhood and early adolescent years? The disaster of him moving in with us at sixteen? The estranged end of high school years? The discovery that my son was in Iraq? His return from war, dishonorable discharge, and PTSD? His marriage, birth of our first grandson, and jailing of the little man's mother shortly after birth? I found some words when I looked around the table, saw the love in the eyes of true friends.

"We don't have a relationship. We've been estranged for many years. Amputated himself from us, completely. It's the most painful thing in my life, trying to talk about my son, trying to understand how . . . how . . . I'm so sorry. I'll be right back," I said. "I just want to get some air," I said as I left the table and went outside.

"Merda (shit)," Valerio said, "I shouldn't have asked anything. I'm sorry."

My husband responded, "Don't worry, John has a difficult time talking about his relationship with his son. Doesn't even talk to me. Except in his sleep."

"What happened?"

"How long has it been?"

"It's difficult to say exactly what happened, it seemed like one minute they were in our life and then they weren't," my husband explained. "His son blames John for all of his pain, all of his suffering. He told his father he wanted nothing to do with him, with us really, that it was useless writing letters, he wouldn't read them. He changed all of his phone numbers, uses a different name on social media so his dad can't find him. I watch John sit every year wiping tears as he addresses birthday cards and Christmas cards. We have no idea if they are opened and read, if our grandson even knows we write. If you ask me, part of John agrees with his son, blames himself for everything."

"No wonder he needed some air," Valerio added. "I'll go check on him."

"Good, you do that while I clear the table a bit and get the *digestivi* out."

The men continued in their positions, chatting, while the women jumped up to help in the kitchen.

Leaning against a tree in the darkness, I soon saw the outline of Valerio approaching.

"John, I'm sorry I brought that up. I had no idea why you never talk about it. So sorry if I hurt you. I didn't know how painful this was for you."

"Valerio, you don't have to apologize for asking the truth," I said. "Let's let it rest for tonight, enjoy the rest of our anniversary. C'mon. I hate talking about it because it is too emotional, as you saw. In time, Vale, in time. I just needed some air. I'm not one to show emotions in front of people."

We hugged and walked back to the party.

Even in the face of love what little I said was enough to keep me in bed awake all night. Again.

I should have listened to my husband. He told me to wear gloves and go slowly when I went into the garden early the next morning. I measured out where to plant, placed small stakes to create a new row on the edge of the gray/green olive grove.

"Chi va piano, va lontano, e arriva sano," my husband reminded from the kitchen window. (He who goes slowly, goes far and arrives healthy.) "You can finish this after lunch. Come in."

Hours later, getting too dark to see, I chuckled as I looked first at my blistered and filthy hands and smiled as I gazed at seven new fruit trees. Trees that will bear fruit long after we are gone. Seven grandchildren growing tall.

Leaning against the old well, I examined the chunk of terra cotta that my day's work had unearthed. One thousand years old? Two thousand? Maybe new? I tossed it aside. My mind wandered in the steel blue twilight. The chorus of time, of changes, that these hills, trees, and rocks could sing. Our time here, nothing in comparison. "Carpe diem quam minimum credula postero" (translation: pluck the day, trusting as little as possible in the next one), the Roman poet Horace once wrote.

Yet, decades together, for better, for worse, for our sons, participants in our life, for my son, who took a different road and left us no directions, I have learned one thing: "To thine own self be true." Authenticity is my home. It seems like yesterday that I was escaping from a Victorian home with three doors, enlisting in the army to get off the streets, watching my son play beside the Christmas tree, my wife assuring me that one day he would understand. It seems I was always leaving, but never arriving, until now.

Wrapped in a violet silence between day and night, in the hills surrounding Rome, the inspiration for many poets, an owl screeches, swoops into the vineyard and disappears. A light is turned on and my husband appears in the kitchen window. "How about calling it a day!" he suggests. I lean my tools against the well, examine the trees one more time, the fruit of our labor, and walk towards our home. Yes, I will "pluck" the day.

UNITED WE STAND

THROUGH THE CRIES OF AN OPIATE ORPHAN

Theresa Quinones/Buccico

When conversations are taboo, wounds never heal. Pain is passed down from ancestors along with physical traits; I can hear the echoing of their souls' cries. To find a home where I could feel at peace, I needed to uncover the past that had been buried with people, some who I'd never met. I needed to discover the family truths that had been tightly wrapped up in secrets and lies. Now my voice, the voice of an opiate orphan, will finally tell the story that heals.

1

I am Theresa, named after the grandmother who raised me from infancy. I will always refer to her as "Ma" and I am forever her "Mija" ("my daughter"), as she called me. Ma filled me up with great memories, like the smell of sofrito when I'm making it as she taught me, and the sound of the songs she played, from Luis Miguel to Bocelli. Although we lived in a basement apartment on Pleasant Street, her love made everything beautiful.

Growing up, I can't forget the lit-up dumpsters in The Valley at night. The orange light created ghostly shapes that floated to the sky. To others, they were simply dumpster fires. To me, they were the project's campfire. If you'd seen me playing in Elm Park or dancing on the stage at the Latin festival of Worcester's Institute Park, you would have seen a happy kid. Until I was eleven, life still had innocence.

2

It only took a four-hour trip to Brooklyn to take away the life I thought was mine. Until that day, I didn't know the feeling of being less than. Until that car ride, I never realized I was not Ma's daughter but her *granddaughter*. This is the story of how I met my biological mother.

Ma is driving the car, and I'm in the back seat. Ma says, "This is my daughter," when introducing the woman she calls "Gigi." She has an angelic glow around her. Her white coat trimmed with white fur on the hood is beautiful. When I finally get the courage to engage her, I call out, "Gigi!" Why do I get reprimanded? She looks at me side-eyed, and with an attitude in her tone says, "I'm your mom." How can this be? I have no memories of her, and yet the feeling in my gut doesn't dispute the truth. I look at her and see dimples on her face that I know from my own.

By the end of that ride, I had grown closer to the painful truth, but it was a truth that brought no healing. She had abandoned me! And each new experience of my birth mother in my youth increased my anger.

I felt anger when I thought about my baby sister, Jasmine, who was born not long after that car ride. And when Jasmine died at ten months, I felt overwhelmed with pain. I had made my baby sister smile, held her little body, and played with her. I couldn't understand why she was gone. Now I know she was infected with HIV by my mother at birth. I was in fifth grade. It was my first funeral.

By the time I was fourteen-years old, I was already used to helping Ma clean out apartments after Gigi would disappear again because of drugs. The pain on Ma's face was unforgettable: that look reminded me it wasn't only me Gigi was abandoning. When Ma would say with a shaky voice, "Mija, be careful of needles," I knew she was warning me about something more than getting stabbed while cleaning. But I was never given an explanation. I felt dragged along, cautioned, silenced. But I would always reassure Ma somehow that I understood, making a silent pact that I would not make the same mistakes.

3

By the time I was 17, Ma was aging quickly, and as she declined she began to pass on long-hidden family stories. I was one of seven children born to Gigi, beginning when she was only sixteen. But because she put drugs and alcohol ahead of parenting, Gigi wasn't there for any of us. Listening, I was able to imagine my infant self, left alone by Gigi to scar both physically and emotionally over hours and days. The scars I still have on my right thigh testify to those infant cries. But I could also picture the joy of Ma bringing me home to Massachusetts on a Greyhound bus in 1981 after a painful call from her daughter. Ma said that it was one of the smelliest rides she ever had, but as I lay still in her arms, we both smiled. "It was meant to be, Mija," she'd say. Each time she retold that story, she smiled.

I could hear her pride.

But Gigi, too, had been abandoned by a parent struggling with drug use: her dad. And at the age of eleven Ma, too, had been abandoned along with three younger siblings by her mother, Emilia, back in Humacao, Puerto Rico. This multigenerational cycle shaped Ma's life, Gigi's life, and my own. Despite all the trauma passed down due to abandonment, alcohol, drugs, and mental illness, Teresa Curbelo was able to raise me with love. And that, too, shapes who I am today.

Gigi died in her early forties. Like her father, she was taken by the early '80s inner-city tsunami: HIV infection caused by heroin use with needles. I was only twenty-four years old then, and despite my promises to Ma, I had started down my own path of numbing life's experiences. But my mother's death was the turning point of my life. I would never use drugs again. In a sense, that was Gigi's gift to me.

4

Ma's gift for me was the way she nurtured and loved Gigi, my brother, and me in spite of all that pain. She never gave up on any of her family members. She always prayed and stayed in faith. She taught me it was not my place to take on ancestral pain or behavior patterns. I had the right to rise from the brokenness of the past. She empowered me to live, dream, and love! So I no longer question whose child I am. From the time I was an opiate orphan to the day my flesh becomes one again with the earth, I am and always have been a child of God and Ma's daughter.

Eventually time, like a thief in the night, carried Ma away. I was 35. Now, although Ma is in her eternal Home in heaven, she carries on with me. Her voice in my heart tells me "Mija, I always go before you, to prepare a place for you, so that you may always feel at home."

And I carry on her legacy. With my husband I am raising our two daughters. My oldest daughter carries her grandma's name as her middle name in
English translation—Estrella means Star. And my youngest carries her nickname; we call her Gigi.

5

There was a time in my life when I believed my soul was broken. Looking in
the mirror, I couldn't unsee the reflections of Estrella, Teresa, and Emilia in
myself. Would history repeat in me? Living past the experience of the women
who had come before me would take strategy and strength. Could I do it?

Now, some wounds have healed: I have beautiful scars. Learning and telling the story of intergenerational trauma is the process I'm using to mend
my heart and mind, body and soul. These are no longer the lonely cries of an
opiate orphan, but instead the song of a woman who stands united in memory with her mother, grandmother, and great-grandmother, loving them all
back to life as Ma did for me.

MY GREAT MIGRATION

Louise Burrell

My parents were sharecroppers in Sunflower, Mississippi, and we lived in an old shack on Mr. Thomas's land. The place was so cold and the cracks in the ceiling were so wide that when it would rain we had to put buckets down to catch all the water. On clear nights you could see the sky while you lay in bed.

In the 1960s, people in Mississippi couldn't have slaves anymore, but some people could surely manage to take all your labor and money. You could pick or chop cotton from five thirty in the morning until five thirty in the evening, six days a week. Then you would have to go home and shower and cook for your family and clean your home. As a sharecropper, you had to give half the cotton you grew to the family who owned the land. You also had to use the owner's scales to weigh your crop and the owner's cotton gin to clean the cotton—which meant the owner kept the seeds for the next planting. You even had to sell your crop through the owner's broker. The profit you earned from your work got smaller with each step in the process. The same people who owned the land also rented you the farm equipment and owned all the gas stations and grocery stores. They ended up getting back the little bit of money they paid you when you had to buy necessities.

We weren't the only family that lived on Mr. Thomas's land. There were many other families. Everyone we knew was in search of a better way of life. My aunt was the first one to move north to Worcester, Massachusetts. Later, she came back for her sister. From that point on, my whole extended family went north, one small group at a time. Eventually, it was our turn.

One day, my dad said to my mom: "Mary, let's go. Everyone is ready, and it's time for us to put the kids in this old truck. We're heading to Massachusetts!

Tell your mama and daddy we'll be back as soon as we can for the rest of the kids." Eventually my dad said, "Mary, wake up! We're here. This is our new apartment for now, but it won't be long as we'll be in our own home. We're going to work hard and make that happen."

I was just two years old at the time of the move. My younger sister was the baby, and my brother Sam was a year older than me. We are the ones that came with my parents. We were the youngest; the older ones had to stay behind and wait for my parents to return for them. This is how it was for the people coming from the South.

After my other brothers and sisters made it here, we were ready to begin our new lives in Worcester. My parents were hard workers, and just like they said, two years after we had arrived, we were moving into our new home. My dad decided he wanted to be a landlord, so he bought a three-family house and we moved into the first floor.

My dad worked as a special police officer for the Chicago Beef Company, and my mom worked at Brown Shoe. On my dad's days off he would take us all out to the park or to a fishing hole or the beach. The summers were the best. My dad would make us homemade snow cones and ice cream. Oh, the tastes of those treats still dance in my mind!

You would think a man with fourteen kids wouldn't have time for anything else besides work and family, but not my dad. He was a Mason, and my mom was an Eastern Star. In addition, he was a deacon in our church, and my mom was a deaconess. And my dad also started a charity called Faith, Hope and Charity, which collected clothes for the less fortunate. Clothing was sent all over the world to those who needed it.

Mom was one of the greatest cooks, and our dinner would be ready every day when we came home from school. The smells that would come from her kitchen! She would always call us into the kitchen when she wanted us to learn how to prepare the meal she was making. That was fun, too. If it was a cake, we got to lick the spoon.

Together, my parents taught us important life lessons. God and family came first. Every Sunday, everybody in the house goes to church. If you date a boy, you first bring him home and introduce him to your father. Dad would say yes or no, and if it was yes, the boy had to come to your living room to have the date. If your parents aren't at home, you can't go outside unless you have previous permission. And you keep your room clean.

In 1974 my dad had a stroke that left his left side paralyzed. He was going to have to go to rehab, but the day my dad was leaving the hospital he had a heart attack and didn't make it.

I still remember sitting on that front seat in the church with tears streaming down my face. So many people came to say their goodbyes to my dad for the last time that I could see he meant a lot to a lot of people.

A year after my dad died, we moved from the home our dad had made for us to a five-bedroom apartment, and there my mom did her best to make sure we had all we needed. I can say the love and lessons that were shared in our home will never be forgotten.

I'll never forget all the things my father and mother did for others, and I'm glad some of that rubbed off on me. For example, my mother was very involved in doing work for our church. As a deaconess, she had a major role in church affairs, and she had a special place to sit during services every Sunday. Because of her influence, I decided to become a Sunday school teacher when I was only twelve years old. The late Reverend T. Hargrove was so impressed that he arranged for me to receive an award from the city. It made my mother very proud.

Mom was a very soft-spoken woman who always showed her kindness for others. Everywhere she went, everyone loved her. But she also had remarkable strength. With only a ninth-grade education, my mom decided she wanted to get her GED—and she did. She also started her own home daycare and ran it until 2007.

Even without Dad helping, she worked hard to move the family forward. One day Mrs. Betty Price called my mom and said: "Mrs. Burrell, your daughter is turning sixteen, and we would like for her to be a debutante. If you accept, she will be groomed to take her place in society, and she will be introduced to the public at a formal ball." My mother said yes, and from that point on I had my hands full. I had to pick a role model and write an essay about how she inspired me. My model was Harriet Tubman. We also had to learn how to set a proper table and how to waltz. The best part for me was wearing a long white gown with long white gloves. Because I was so tall I had to wear ballerina slippers instead of heels. It was a night I'll never forget, nor will I ever forget Mrs. Elizabeth "Betty" Price, who made all this happen. I was only the second black debutante in Worcester.

If my parents hadn't had the courage to leave their home in Sunflower,

Mississippi, all those years earlier, my life would have been very different. After all, Sunflower County was infamous for the way it treated African Americans. It was the home of Parchman State Prison, where the Freedom Riders were jailed. The barn where Emmett Till was killed was also in Sunflower County. My parents never talked to me about Emmett Till—but I'm sure that's why they never let me or my siblings go south to visit my grandparents. Even though they had been brought up in a place that tried to teach them they were worthless, the members of my family proudly marched with Martin Luther King. And I think the same strength that allowed them to march is what allowed my mother and father to move our family north— get jobs, join organizations, establish a foundation, and help their family and neighbors build better lives.

When my mother died in 2020, my long white debutante dress was still hanging in my mother's closet. I think it always reminded her of how far we'd come from the sharecropper's shack in Sunflower, Mississippi.

MY GRANDFATHER'S GARDEN

Murtaza Akbari

When I was a child, my grandfather had a beautiful garden. In the summer the garden was full of colors as flowers bloomed and fruit ripened.

Apricots were my favorite, but those trees were so tall that I couldn't reach the fruit when I was little. So my grandfather would help me grab the fruits, and I would enjoy their amazingly sweet taste. I always thought they tasted better than anything I'd ever eaten because my grandfather took such care of his garden.

I always loved to help my grandfather plant and water his trees, and he would use our time together to teach me how I should plant my own garden in the future when I grew up.

My grandfather and grandmother also taught me it was important to get an education. They wanted me to understand the world around me and be able to solve problems. One of the biggest problems in my home country, Afghanistan, is that people are not knowledgeable, they don't know how to read and write. The generation before me didn't go to school because of the war. My own generation got an education because of reforms that didn't last. Now girls can't go to school, and the boys don't have good teachers.

It is summer now; my grandfather's garden must be blooming. But my grandfather and I aren't there to enjoy it together. He died, and I left my country to come to America so I could use my education by being a journalist and writing the truth.

But I will carry on my grandfather's tradition here in my new home. I will continue my education so I can help build a better world, and I will plant a garden to make the land green and useful for the generations to come. And each time I reach up in my garden to grab an apricot, I will remember my grandmother and my grandfather, and the garden where I learned how to become the man I am today.

MY MOTHER AND GEORGE FLOYD

Donna Evans

The day of George Floyd's funeral I was homebound and feeling vulnerable. I'd just entered into remission from cancer and was still battling a number of medical issues. These conditions made me a high-risk patient who couldn't risk going out during the pandemic. That's why I was home in my bedroom on the day of the funeral.

Like most people, I never liked going to funerals, yet I respect the value of them as a way to honor the dead and instruct the living. This is one funeral I would never have missed. Even though I was alone in my bedroom, I felt at one with the countless others who were watching and rewatching the video of George Floyd's death, and who kept up the "No Justice, No Peace" demonstrations.

As Reverend Al Sharpton began delivering the eulogy, I felt myself merge with and embrace the other mourners at the funeral. I remembered myself as a child watching the funerals of John F. Kennedy and Dr. Martin Luther King. I realized there was a common thread.

As Reverend Sharpton walked us through the journey of George Floyd's life, I thought, "Wait! This journey sounds familiar." Yes, my family and I had many negative experiences growing up in Black and Brown communities.

During my childhood, my family struggled financially and I ended up in the projects—"subsidized housing." Instead of a welcome basket when we moved into the neighborhood, we got a message written on our sidewalk, "Niggers go back." Someone had dumped food on our walkway as well. Over and over again I watched my family struggle against prejudice, racism, and social injustice, whether it was in housing, employment, or education.

And yet, my mother was an independent, god-fearing woman who raised us to be respectful and responsible on every level. She knew what responsibility was—her parents had thirteen children and she had helped raise her siblings. Yet, no matter how hard she worked, she was always kind and loved to speak to everyone.

One day she went to the bank to cash her check and then go to the local convenience store. At the cash register she paid for her items with the hundred-dollar bill she got at the bank. The clerk informed her that her money was counterfeit. My mother explained where she got the bill and the clerk told her to go back to the bank, but he kept her money. When my mom called me, she was upset by the incident and angry that the clerk stole her money. When I look back, I feel bad for my mom—but then I realize that George Floyd's story could have been my mom's story.

These problems aren't over. There have been days I've been stopped like a cheap watch—every second. I've worked at places where people would walk by me every day and not say hello. You're wondering why I didn't go to human resources? It's that privilege thing. Often the person who was the problem was a friend of the human resources director. As a result, I've lived with countless acts of blatant disrespect.

That's why it felt like Reverend Sharpton was speaking for me and my mother and all the people in the Black and Brown community when he said at the funeral:

> We are not fighting some disconnected incidents. We are fighting an institutional, systemic problem that has been allowed to permeate since we were brought to these shores and we are fighting wickedness in high places. When you can put your knee on a man's neck and hold it there for 8 minutes and 46 seconds, that's not even normal to a civilian, less known to a police officer. Try it when you go home to put your knee down on something and hold it there that long. You got to be full of a lot of venom. Full of something that really motivates you to press down your weight that long and not give up. . . . George Floyd's story has been the story of black folks because ever since 401 years ago, the reason we could never be who we wanted and dreamed to be is you kept your knee on our neck.

Hearing those words, remembering those pains, made me feel sad, and tired, and angry as the day went on. But I knew I couldn't be so discouraged that I gave up. I remembered that Martin Luther King told us:

If you can't fly, run;
If you can't run, walk;
If you can't walk, crawl;
But by all means keep moving.

And suddenly Reverend Sharpton's words cut through my thinking, reminding me of the simple truth of how we can all move forward together.

Jesus told the story that there was a man laying by the side of the road. He'd been robbed and beaten. They said one man came by that was his same race, his fellow brother, and he kept walking. Then another man came by that was steeped and well-read in the scriptures. Knew every scripture, knew how to quote the book back and forward. But he only quoted the book, he never lived by the book. And he kept walking. But Jesus said a third man came by and he stopped and looked at the man. He wasn't the same race, wasn't the same religion. But he picked the man up and he took care of restoring the man to his rightful being. And Jesus called him the Good Samaritan. The problem is too many of you have been walking by the Eric Garners, been walking by the Trayvon Martins, been walking by the Arberys, been walking by. And now we stopped for George Floyd.

Depending on who you are, watching the video of George Floyd dying may or may not remind you of your own mother or brother or husband or father. But the Bible reminds us that the Good Samaritan stopped for the man who wasn't the same race or same religion. It's a simple story with a powerful truth. Why not make this the beginning of a new age of Good Samaritans?

THE ONE THAT KILLED

Brian K. Johnson

My parents were both in the service of the United States Army. My mom, Loretta V. M. Johnson, was a young student teacher who had just graduated from school. She found a job teaching the enlisted men in the US Army to read and write. There is a black-and-white picture showing my mom, looking young with dark, shiny skin, sitting on a fence in the sun, wearing a scarf to wrap her hair, a button-down shirt with cuffs rolled up, and khaki or light color pants.

My dad, Harold E. Johnson, appears in another photograph I have, standing tall, light skinned, smiling, smoking in a doorway that looks like a kitchen back door. He wore some kind of paper cap on his head, dressed in his army uniform covered with an apron. Dad was a cook and a master of fixing things with his hands, especially food.

Me? I went to school, education classes for reading, writing, and math. I had trouble with reading and pronunciation. My first years of education weren't normal. My mom, a teacher herself, had the school keep me back one year. Loretta and Harold showed me extra attention, with puzzles and construction kits I had to put together. Harold was heavy on keeping me busy.

Both of my parents smoked cigarettes. It was the '70s when lots of adults did. When they were not minding me, they would go off to another part of the house and smoke. As much as Denice, Beverly, Olivia—my sisters—and I tried, we could not get them to stop the cigarettes.

So we worked on my mom first by hiding her smokes, wetting the matches, and flushing her smokes down the toilet. Loretta was smart, and onto what was happening, so as much as the family tried, we were losing with our efforts. As time went on mom would hide the smokes from us. It is not easy for parents to listen to you when you're young. During those years, parents expected children to sit and not speak unless spoken to. Those were only some of the rules. There was a whole dictionary of rules.

Finally Loretta admitted defeat and gave up her smokes. On a day when the whole family was happy, my mom brought us together at dinner, after we had returned from church, to give us the news that she was making up her own mind. "I decided to stop smoking," she said, like she had made that up all by herself.

Now Harold, however, was not going to be easy; he was hard to move. I remember another family member asking when it would be his turn to quit smoking. He replied, "It's like taking one of my children. You won't be getting my smokes." Dad, standing six foott six and more in height, smiled a lot, but he also had a very serious side that could stop a bus in its tracks.

My dad would come and go, while keeping me busy; he would buy me Erector sets and other things so I could keep busy and put things together with my hands. He always kept his smokes out of view, not smoking in the house. It sure was not going to be easy getting him to quit his other child, smoking, without making him upset. I would search and search, but all I could find were ashes and ashtrays. So I hid the ashtrays, though that was risky too, if he caught me. Our campaign to get Harold to stop smoking went on for a while. I searched the spare room that was used because my parents were foster parents. They had a desk and a daybed for guests, and so when the room was not being used, my dad made it his office. I found lots of things he hid in that room, like beer and alcohol, but I did not find smokes. At times I drove my dad crazy by searching and not giving up. While looking for the smokes I got into everything else he had. I made an adventure of it all as a child. The search was both fun and dangerous.

Harold loved his children (the other one was his smokes). For me, he could express how he felt by giving gifts and paying attention, showing love as much as a man could during that time, when men were supposed to keep their emotions to themselves. Men were men, and in the '70s could only express minimal feelings, except with family and real close friends. Until this day, men, especially Black men and men of color, still face this issue.

Time went on. I was always looking for the cigarettes. My dad was at the top of his game. He never smoked in the house. I got into trouble a few times for tinkering and taking apart his things, but the other child (smokes) remained, was the smell of smoke.

In my ESL class we read *Highlight* magazines, Dr. Seuss books, and lots of math practice sheets. My mom taught at the Joseph Hurley School in Boston, and Dad went to work doing maintenance in downtown Boston at the JFK building. We were happy, but Mom and Dad were quiet. Dad started to be home more. A child never knows the weight an adult carries. Mom and Dad worked hard in the '70s to provide for their family, always trying to do better in life.

One day when I was eleven years old, I came home from school doing my usual—getting into things, bouncing around the house, watching TV, doing homework. Then the phone rang loudly. That old thing had never sounded so clear. I ignored the first few rings of the phone. I was the only one home, so eventually I had to answer it. A voice on the other end asked for my mother.

"Is Loretta there?" the voice asked.

I replied, "No, she is not home now. Can I take a message?" At eleven, I knew that being polite on the phone was a good idea. I never knew if it was a relative on the other end who would tell my mom or dad. The person on the phone said the message was that Harold, her husband, requires her attention at the hospital as soon as she can get there. I was like, a hospital?

The next day I stayed home from school. I was having fun running around, never thinking about a thing, till mom came in the door looking sad and upset. "What's wrong, Mom?" I asked her.

"He's gone!"

"Who?" I replied.

Mom exclaimed, "Your dad has died in the hospital from cancer with complications of pneumonia. Now you're the man of the house. You need to grow up," mom said. "You're the man of the house," she said again, with tears. The thought sank in slowly. Many meanings rushed through my head, as to a child back then, death was unusual, strange, different.

The disconnect comes from adults not knowing how to explain things to children clearly so they can grasp the meaning of big events like death, even though it might take a while for them to understand fully. I don't remember much of the funeral. Being young at that time did not mean I could not have understood death. Young humans can understand bigger things. It's the concept of explaining it as an adult to a child so they can clearly hear what is being said, even though it may take a while, that matters. I have blocked out some things about that encounter until this day. What I do have is a memory of him, Harold, and the things and people he left behind—my mom, sisters, extended family, and me, his son. But I'm not the one who killed him. The other child—smoking—did.

A STORY OF MOM AND HOME

George Thorney

I was the only one of my mother's six children to live with her in childhood. We lived in a wooden seven by ten room in an urban village in Jamaica. There was no electricity or running water. But even though our life was hard, my mother always made sure that our home was a place of warmth and togetherness.

My older sister and three of my older brothers lived with their fathers or my maternal grandmother so that my mother could go out to work and help support us. The brother closest to me in age contracted an eye condition that left him legally blind. I remember him being shipped off to a boarding school for children with vision problems.

However, my mother kept me with her because I was the youngest and because she felt I needed special nurturing. At the age of just four months, I'd contracted polio, and although I hadn't been paralyzed, I had been left with serious disabling conditions. I have vivid memories of her fierce and loving determination to instill a sense of pride in me. Thanks to her, I grew up with a sense of confidence.

Certainly, my mother's entrepreneurial efforts made her a great role model. She started by cleaning other people's houses and taking care of other people's children. But later she began to sell peanuts on the streets as well as hard-boiled eggs, offering people salt and pepper to season them before eating. Eventually, she set up a stall where she sold boiled corn on the cob, nubbly or spiky-skinned breadfruit the size of volleyballs, boiled crabs, and roasted yellow yams with salted codfish topped with onions, cucumbers, tomatoes, and fiery hot peppers. Every morning she'd roll her two-wheeled cart to the stand and set up her cook stove and pots and pans. Every night, she'd put everything back in the cart and wheel it home.

The confidence I learned from my mother was useful when I went to school. Polio meant that I couldn't do a lot of the things my peers could do. For example, although I loved sports, I couldn't play soccer. Once there was a raffle in school, and the big prize was a leather soccer ball. I won. With my mother's encouragement, I would take the ball to school every Friday and let the other guys play with it. One week while I was watching them, I became overwhelmed by the feeling of being left out. I demanded the ball back, went home in tears, and threw the ball under the bed. But at times like that, my mother would always be encouraging.

I think the spirit I got from my mother helped me get a group of friends who looked up to me and were always protective and supportive. Whenever I had a need, I would just say to my friends, "I need to . . ." and at least two or three guys would step up and say, "Let me do it for you!" They would fight over getting to do things for me. Even today people continue to look up to me and do things for me, and I'm glad to have them in my life.

But just as friends help me, I always help others because my mom taught me the value of giving. She believed that when you have a need, you should give out of your need. For example, if you have a hundred dollars and someone asks for ten, you should give it freely. Then when you get to the store where you were going to buy a hundred-dollar suit, you should strike a deal to get it for ninety. Somehow, my mother taught me, it will all work out.

And it is this belief in myself, in my friends, and in giving that stays with me today and makes me feel at home even though I'm many miles from that seven by ten room on an island in the middle of the blue Caribbean.

YEARS IN A LIFE

William Murphy

My favorite combat position was prone by an ancient elm tree that, despite the exposed roots digging into my skinny ribcage, afforded perfect sightlines and shooting angles. An adjacent stockade fence provided both cover from detection and shade from the searing sun. Typically, the tarmac straight ahead was clear of any vehicles or machinery to obstruct my shots. The dense Old World forest and vegetation twenty yards to the rear were my sole escape route to a stream that I could easily ford or speed down in a raft hidden a short distance downstream. I had used this position successfully many times on selected human targets. On other operations I used the same basic procedures without fail. I did my homework, I practiced, I was patient, I was equipped, and, most importantly, I wanted to succeed. I was not going to just go through the motions.

Most operations ended the same way. "Billy, Joey! Time for dinner."

Once in a while, an operation ended when the intended target, my brother Joey, claimed he shot and killed me first when he hadn't. In those instances, the game degenerated into a yelling match—or more—with mutual declarations to never play again. The statute of limitations on those claims covered the period until the next sunrise.

Both my parents were World War II veterans. Dad was an army tank commander under General Patton in the Battle of the Bulge. Mom operated Morse code for the navy. After the war they went to work for the Veterans Administration where they met, got married, and moved into a second-floor walkup apartment at the corner of Columbia Road and Blue Hill Avenue. I was baptized at St. Hughes in Grove Hall. In 1950, the Dorchester Murphys, with two sons in tow, moved into a two-bedroom Cape Cod–style house (purchased with a VA-backed loan) on Rockcroft Road, a dead-end street in Weymouth. Mom's mother, Ma Mulligan from Roxbury, moved into the dining room, thus converting the house to a three bedroom.

Rockcroft was one of many rural streets that were reshaped into small lots to accommodate the families of war veterans such as Bill Murphy and Ann Mulligan Murphy. Across the street was a meadow and a field and a forest. In sight of 39 Rockcroft Road were two abandoned stone buildings, the remnants of a farmhouse with two and a half walls and part of its chimney beckoning curious kids. Some type of watering hole for farm animals, with a cobbled slope surrounded by stone retaining walls, provided a setting for games of cowboys and the like. The structures were now overgrown with waist-high grasses and a sparse mixture of young seedlings, long-dead tree trunks, and two mature apple trees. This landscape provided venues for contests of tag and hide-and-seek that kept children busy and often late for dinner.

As a dead-end street, Rockcroft was home field to continuous stickball, touch football, and street hockey games. Behind our house was Mill River, composed more of pools of standing water interspersed with slowly moving rivulets—ten feet at its widest, four feet at its deepest. The smell was more akin to a swamp than a river, but it was upstream from the lumber mill. Still, at that spot and at that time in history, it was free of pollutants. Hardly Twain's *Life on the Mississippi*, but it was the scene of many gambols and gambles. During the postwar housing boom, masons on the nearby housing subdivision project were aggravated when their cement mixing tubs went missing, appropriated for riverboat duty by Rockcroft boatmen. No matter what activity was afoot, Mill River was more often than not the scene of noncriminal violations of the come-home-for-dinner, don't-get- your-pants-wet, no-throwing-rocks, don't-play-with-matches regulations in force at the time.

My parents continued their government service with Dad a mailman for the US Post Office and Mom a clerk for the US Department of Defense. Commuting into Boston each day, they took a chance that leaving latchkey kids at home in the suburbs was safer than Mom staying at home and letting her two boys out on the streets of Dorchester. Dad clearly intended to shield his two sons from the inconveniences and horrors that he had encountered in the war. He strongly preached that we should not join the armed services— certainly not as a draftee, infantry, or enlisted man. Mom, in her typical reserved manner, subtly got across her message that she considered military service a monumental waste of time and life—although considered necessary in her time. They both did their best to guard us from the dangers lurking beyond Rockcroft Road. They both nurtured us toward pursuing a college education and public service.

As Greenwich Village folksinger Dave Van Ronk wrote, "We were having the time of our lives. We were hanging out with our friends . . . and we were laughing all the time."[6]

* * *

In June 1963, President John F. Kennedy forwarded landmark civil rights legislation to Congress. In June 1963, he also gave what the *Boston Globe* called his most important speech, "A Strategy for Peace" at American University in Washington, DC.

I decided to go to American University.

Hubie and I lived together for two years in the dorm at American University in Washington, DC, before he married his childhood sweetheart in 1969. In our senior year, December 1969, our postgraduate plans were interrupted by the draft lottery. In what could have been our last summer, the summer of 1970, Hubie and I, induced by the draft[7] and by the desire to avoid assignment to the infantry, enlisted in the US Army Security Agency Language Program, hoping for a career-advancing and life-prolonging language such as French or Italian or even more Latin (I had studied four years), Instead, I got Vietnamese, Saigon dialect. With similar aspirations, especially as a newlywed, Hubie got Vietnamese, Hanoi/north dialect. We spent the remainder of 1970 together in basic training at Fort Dix and the full calendar year 1971 at the Defense Language Institute, Fort Bliss, Texas. All the while we hoped the war would end soon.

Unsurprisingly, after the completion of the forty-seven-week intensive Vietnamese language course, Hubie and I received orders for Viet Nam. Hubie and his new wife went to Toronto.

I went home to Weymouth for thirty days' leave before shipping out.

---

[6] Dave Van Ronk, *The Mayor of MacDougal Street* (Cambridge, MA: DaCapo Press, 2005), 213.
[7] A term developed by Christian Appy, *Patriots* (New York: Viking, 2003).

Since 1969, the United States had been giving increased battle responsibility to the Republic of Viet Nam's Army (ARVN). Officials called this the "Vietnamization of the war." Critics called it the Vietnamization of the caskets. American troops were being sent home. During the period of February to April 1972, over fifty-eight thousand returned home, the largest troop withdrawal of the war. That left only about sixty-nine thousand American troops in Viet Nam, many of whom made up only two combat brigades and a reduced air force presence. During the period 1966–71, the "net body count" in the war was drastically in the favor of the American and South Vietnamese forces. In mid-1971 that kill ratio swung in the favor of the Viet Cong (VC)/ North Vietnamese Army (NVA) and continued until January 1973, when the peace treaty was signed.

Wait, I was about to leave home for a war zone that has just experienced the largest American troop *withdrawal* of the war, and, at the same time, the enemy—who by all accounts was already winning—began what was described as the *fiercest* campaign of the war.

The ARVN was losing a regiment a month to AWOLs and desertions. One American wrote home from Viet Nam, "There's no reason to be here and there is even less reason to see Americans dying here."[8]

On March 10, 1972, the intrepid 101st Airborne Division drew down from Viet Nam, a poignant signal.

On March 19, 1972, the US bombing of the Ho Chi Min Trail intensified.

On March 23, 1972, the Paris peace talks were suspended.

On March 30, 1972, at about noon, NVA regular units, not surreptitious insurgents, invaded across the demilitarized zone separating North and South Viet Nam, and by April 2, 1972, South Viet Nam hero Colonel Pham Van Dinh surrendered, shocking the rest of the ARVN. By April 23, 1972, the North accomplished incredible victories primarily due to "insufficient and inadequate supply, deficiency in intelligence and tardy deployment of the reserves . . . [the] ARVN leadership was most lacking."[9] During one battle, an ARVN tank was moved to respond to a nearby NVA roadblock; seeing the tank leave, thinking the worst, panic set in among the ARVN troops who fled.

---

[8] Bernard Edelman, ed., *Dear America: Letters Home from Vietnam.* Vietnam Veterans Commission (New York: W.W. Norton, 1985) Letter dated July 2, 1970, 227–28.

[9] Albert Grandolini, *The Easter Offensive Vietnam 1972*, vol. 1 (West Midlands, England: Helion, 2015), 33.

One of the ten most important battles of the war in Viet Nam, the North's Easter Offensive, sought to capture Saigon and end the idiotic, multinational, multicentury futility of the American colonial project. The focus of the North Vietnamese strategy was the Saigon–Long Binh–Bien Hoa corridor, a mission similar to the Tet Offensive of 1968. Using the maximum number of NVA military forces, and after considering the Vietnamization of the war in the south and the political climate in the United States, NVA General Vo Nguyen Giap was optimistic that a final march to Saigon would be successful.

Cam Ranh Bay, an R&R resort and site of Bob Hope shows, was known as "about the safest place you could be in April 1972."[10] On April 9, 1972, the Communists attacked Cam Ranh, killing four Americans and wounding twenty. Three days earlier, the last American combat infantry unit had stood down.

On April 28, 1972, at 0315 hours, while on Mission Number F2A3 on the Flying Tiger Airline and Alaska Airlines, respectively, I checked two baggage pieces totaling sixty-five pounds, and, having been assigned seat number 18, I boarded the flight, destination SGN—Saigon. "On 28 April, the North Vietnamese moved in for their final assault on the now encircled Quang Tri—and panicked civilians began to stream south along Route 1 which was hit indiscriminately, killing thousands of innocent people along the 'Terror Boulevard.'"[11] In April and May 1972, the NVA pressed a third attack according to the plan to gain Saigon. On April 28, 1972, the day I arrived in Viet Nam, Sergeant Franklin East, First Cavalry, from McComas, West Virginia, died at Bien Hoa airbase, twenty miles north of Saigon. Also on that day, Warrant Officer William Allen Haines Jr. from Warren, Ohio, and Captain Paul Vaughan Martindale from Letohatchee, Alabama, of the Fourth Cav First Aviation Brigade died in a helicopter crash in Quang Tri province and Master Sergeant Roy J. Day of the Vung Tau Army HQ Command from Racine, Missouri, died in Phuoc Tuy province.

I was billeted at Davis Station on Tan Son Nhut Airbase, assigned to the 509th Radio Research Group of the Army Security Agency. One of my former language students, "OJ" Johnson, who had arrived months before me, informed me unofficially that the "VC was kickin' ass and taking names." Officially, I learned of the dire battles of An Loc and Quang Tri. I heard the

---

[10] Jim Smith, *Heroes to the End: An Army Correspondents Last Days in Vietnam* (Bloomington, IN: iUniverse, 2015), 239.

[11] Grandolini, *The Easter Offensive*, 34.

CIA analysis that Saigon survived only because of the intensive air force bombing operations. I learned of some heroic ARVN last stands.

In my first two weeks, there were fifty-nine deaths, thirty-five of which were in nearby Bien Hoa province. In the first month there were eighty total in country.

On June 8, 1972, in Trang Bang, "the girl in the picture" had her clothes melted into her back by napalm dropped by her own country's air force, another tragic absurdity in the continuing absurd tragedy that was the war. The photo of Kim Phuc has become famous, but to me the just as compelling image is the face of the boy in the left foreground of the photo looking forward in abject terror. Kim's cousins, an infant and a three-year-old, were also killed. No children should be victims to that inhumanity. No children should witness that. Not by their own people. Not by any people.

On June 9, 1972, the fabled John Paul Vann, military war hero and civilian director of the Agency for International Development, senior advisor for Region II, Pleiku, died in a helicopter crash in Pleiku, enroute to celebrate with troops the victory in holding back NVA at Kontum. Vann, although a civilian, directed artillery and air strikes that saved Kontum. When Vann, the hero of *A Bright Shining Lie*, died, I realized no one was immune.

On June 17, 1972, a group of burglars ransacked an office in Watergate, answering one of singer Country Joe McDonald's most important questions, "What are we fightin' for?" with the obvious answer, "Don't ask me, I don't give a damn."

In August 1972, the last ground troops left Viet Nam.

On July 7, 1972, Staff Sergeant Thomas Patrick Keogh, from Philadelphia, 146th Aviation Company, 509th Radio Research Group, my unit, died in Bien Hoa.

The Easter Offensive lasted up to September 15, 1972, when Quang Tri was saved from the NVA attacks but was reduced to dust. Not rubble, dust. It wasn't until September 30, 1972, that combat operations decreased and another month into October until the area was secured. On November 11, 1972, the United States lowered the American flag at Long Binh and turned the base over to the ARVN. At the time there was a relentless Viet Cong push to influence the Paris peace talks. While living at Davis Station we had two rocket attacks.

On January 1, 1973, my childhood hero Roberto Clemente died in a plane crash while involved in the airlift of supplies to victims of an earthquake in

Nicaragua. It was not lost on me that the upcoming Tet holiday had become a time of VC and NVA military actions.

On January 22, 1973, LBJ died peacefully at his ranch in Texas.

On January 23, 1973, the Paris Peace Accords were signed with the provision that US troops leave Vietnam within sixty days, by the end of March.

I had met the admission requirements of Bill Mauldin's Benevolent and Protective Brotherhood of Them What Has Been Shot At.[12] Fortunately, I didn't meet the criteria of the Benevolent and Protective Brotherhood of Them What Has Been Shot. Thank Christ.

On February 23, 1973, Spec Five James Leland Scroggins, 18th Aviation Co, 164th Aviation Group, First Aviation Brigade, from Mulberry Grove, Illinois, became the last army aviation casualty who died, seven days after a helicopter crash on a supply mission for peacekeeping forces in Binh Long province. He also became the last death before all troops left Viet Nam by March 31, 1973,

On February 23, 1973, I left Viet Nam, a few weeks before the official end of American combat operations. There were no American deaths from the day I left through the end of the pullout at the end of March.

At the Vietnam Veterans Memorial, "The Wall," a flag is flown twenty-four hours a day overlooking the area; at the base are the seals of the five branches of service with the inscription

THIS FLAG REPRESENTS THE SERVICE RENDERED TO OUR COUNTRY BY THE VETERANS OF THE VIETNAM WAR. THE FLAG AFFIRMS THE PRINCIPLES OF FREEDOM FOR WHICH THEY FOUGHT AND THEIR PRIDE IN HAVING SERVED UNDER DIFFICULT CIRCUMSTANCES.

The first casualty of the Viet Nam War was from Weymouth, listed on panel 52E, line 21. The Department of Defense considers the first advisors relative to hostilities in Viet Nam to have begun service on November 1, 1955..One of those advisors was Air Force Technical Sergeant Richard Bernard Fitzgibbon Jr., a World War II Purple Heart recipient and Weymouth resident. On June 8, 1956, Technical Sergeant Richard Bernard Fitzgibbon Jr., 1173rd Foreign MSN Squadron, MAAGV, was handing out candy to kids in Saigon when a deranged fellow American airman shot and killed him, panel 52E, line 21. In my mind, Fitzgibbon the Elder's legacy is as much

---

[12] Bill Mauldin, *Up Front* (New York: Henry Holt, 1945), 100.

based upon how he died—causality officially "homicide"—as opposed to the chronological order of his death, the first, relative to the 58,315 or so others, killed while helping children, an allegory of the idiocy. Sadly, on September 7, 1965, Fitzgibbon's son, Lance Corporal Richard Bernard Fitzgibbon III, Weymouth High School Class of '62, Third Marine Division, III MAF, was killed in Quang Tri from an explosive device, two weeks before he was scheduled to come home, panel 2E, line 77. This unfortunate event made them one of three American father-son pairs killed in Viet Nam. Richard B. Fitzgibbon Jr. and his son Richard B. Fitzgibbon III are buried in the Blue Hills Cemetery in Braintree, where both my father and mother are buried in the military veterans section, as are my good friends US Marshal Billy Degan, killed at Ruby Ridge, and Braintree Police Lieutenant Greg Principe, killed on duty.

Specialist Four James Thomas ("Tom") Davis, radio direction finder operator, Third Radio Research Unit (later the 509th Radio Research Group, my unit), Army Security Group, MAAGV, from Livingston, Tennessee, died as a result of small arms fire on December 22, 1961, in Hau Nghia province, panel 1E, line 4. On January 10, 1962, President Johnson cited Davis as the first battlefield casualty of the Viet Nam War. Davis Station, the Saigon site of at the time approximately ninety troops, became the first military installation in Viet Nam named for a fallen serviceman.

Between my first and last days in Viet Nam, over five hundred American servicemen died. In a way, a young man from Weymouth was in Viet Nam when the first serviceman was killed in the war and when the last was killed in the country before all troops left by March 31, 1973. Dalton Trumbo, in his addendum to the introduction of *Johnny Got His Gun*,[13] stated, "If the dead mean nothing to us, what of the 300,000 wounded? . . . How many arms, legs, ears, noses, mouths, faces, penises they've lost?"

The bullets were as deadly as the rockets' glare was red.

"Servicemen from Dorchester were four times more likely to die in Vietnam than those raised in fancy suburbs."[14]

"The latter stages of American involvement in Vietnam largely have been ignored. . . . There were only 759 American deaths in 1972."[15] *Only.*

---

[13] Dalton Trumbo, *Johnny Got His Gun* (New York: Bantam Books, 1970).
[14] Lois P. Rudnick, ed. *American Identities: An Introductory Textbook* (New York: Wiley, 2005), 139, quoting Christian G. Appy, *Working Class War.*
[15] Smith, *Heroes to the End*, vii.

As Liam Clancy sang about the horrors of the 1915 Battle of Gallipoli in "And the Band Played Waltzing Matilda," "the living just tried to survive."[16]

Daniel Ellsberg said we weren't on the wrong side; we *were* the wrong side.

In his 1996 song, "When a Soldier Makes It Home" (from the album *Mystic Journey*), Arlo Guthrie sang:

Halfway around the world tonight

In a strange and foreign land
A soldier unpacks memories
That he saved from Vietnam

The night is coming quickly
And the stars are on their way
As I stare into the evening
Looking for the words to say

That I saw the lonely soldier
Just a boy that's far from home.[17]

* * *

Doing what I was supposed to do—appreciating the great opportunity to live and work and study in Washington, DC, to develop plans for the next stages of my life—I had seven years taken from me by my government without just cause. I did not give up. I did not try to kill it to save it. I joined the very government—not a deep state, but a flawed government—to which I devoted thirty-four years. I turned two and a half years of *servitude*—servitude enforced and supported by lies of the government—into decades of *service* to my country, saving countless lives and helping fellow Americans flourish according to promises made centuries ago by their government.

Since 1973, the year I left Viet Nam, the panels on a wall at the entrance to JFK's Presidential Library have exhibited a number of his most inspiring quotations. The first words displayed are from his American University

---

[16] Liam Clancy, music and lyrics by Eric Bogle, *"And the Band Played Waltzing Matilda"* (Larrikin Music Ply Limited, Sydney, Australia, 2000).

[17] Arlo Guthrie, *"When a Soldier Makes It Home"* (BMG Rights Management, 1999). USA Today, "Man in Iconic OKC Bombing Photo Breaks Silence," April 23, 2015.

speech—ahead of the most memorable seventeen-word exhortation ("Ask not what your country can do for you . . .") from his Inaugural Address: "Every person sent out from a university should be of his or her nation as well as of his or her time, and I am confident that the men and women who carry the honor of graduating from this institution will continue to give from their lives, from their talents, a high measure of public service and public support."

More than three decades later, I had tickets for an American Airlines flight from Logan Airport, Boston, Massachusetts, to George Bush International in Houston, Texas.

Usually the room in Plymouth, Massachusetts, was set up as a small family restaurant run by the two brothers Donovan and Patrick, who alternated cooking and waiting on tables. Tonight, though, the boys had fashioned an aisle of two rows of chairs and the Fisher-Price toy kitchen as a jet cockpit ready for takeoff instead of the usual food preparation. Donovan was pilot and Patrick copilot for this flight, each outfitted with one of Daddy's official-looking scally caps. Their toy washing machine became the airliner's control panel. There was only one window seat. After dutifully storing their luggage (actual Spiderman rolling suitcases used during their last trip to Texas) and checking my ticket (a receipt from the Massachusetts Lottery Megabucks), they took off. Well, barely took off, until Patrick added two AAA batteries to the long line of batteries Donovan had unsuccessfully added to the engine compartment to increase power.

When Donovan told me we were going from Boston to California to Texas, I questioned why I had booked this flight. He motioned to the nearby GPS (a globe from his desk) and said we were not going *there*, pointing to China. There was mention of Mars and asteroids.

We had a pretty safe flight until copilot Patrick got up to pee and, shortly thereafter, his pilot Donovan also got up to follow. As a nervous flier, I yelled, "Hey, hey, where are you going!" I figured it would be a teaching moment, so while they were standing in the aisle, far away from the controls, I asked them sternly, "Do you know why both the pilot and copilot can't get up at the same time?" Without hesitation, Donovan replied, "Yes, because there's only one toilet."

After a very safe landing, we three went up to the bedroom where Bindi was organizing her animal specimens and Bruce was positioning Star Wars guys while Laila and Madison and Amelia were jumping on Nana's bed in violation of the rule: no more *monkeys jumping on the bed*. Donovan and

Patrick separated, one joining Bruce and Bindi and the other joining the girls' group jump. Julia, Leo, Charlotte, and Beckett had not arrived yet.

I stayed for a moment taking in the scene and spontaneously blurted, "I love you kids."

A child's voice found its way out from the laughter, "We love you, too, Grandfather."

On April 23, 2015, Luke Franey, with whom I attended the Federal Law Enforcement Academy, by now the Special Agent in Charge of the United States Department of Justice, Bureau of Alcohol, Tobacco, Firearms, and Explosives, Denver Field Division, reflected twenty years after the murder of children and other civilians at the Murrah Federal Building in Oklahoma City. He told *USA Today*, "Be a better person. Be a better agent. Be a better husband. Be a better dad. Be a better law enforcement officer, try to prevent these events from happening."[18]

---

[18] *USA Today*, "Man in Iconic OKC Bombing Photo Breaks Silence," April 23, 2015.

WHEN LOVE LOOKS LIKE NEGLECT

Doreen Samuels

One

I only have two memories of my mother. One is me sitting in front of her while she combed my hair. The other is her taking me to visit one of her friends when I was five years old. That was the year she left me with my grandmother to go live and work in England.

While I wasn't in need of food or clothing—probably because my mother was sending back money—there was a void in me. Nights were the worst. When I was a little girl in Jamaica, the nights were the worst. Although I'd go to bed with three or four cousins, I'd feel all alone. While they slept, I'd stay awake crying, trying to keep my sniffles quiet so they wouldn't hear me.

During the day, every time I'd see an airplane overhead, I would shout, "My mother is coming to get me." Then I would stand and watch until it disappeared out of sight. Once I realized she wasn't on the plane, I would go into one of my moods.

In those years when I was growing up, no one ever told me they loved me, and I needed to hear my mother say she loved me. But we were too poor to talk on the phone. And my mother never walked back through the airport gate to come and get me.

Two

The present my aunt sent me for my thirtieth birthday was a plane ticket and visa so I could visit her in Canada. So I left my six children in the care of their father—the youngest was one—and went for a brief vacation.

But once I was there, I kept noticing all the work opportunities. I thought if I stayed awhile, I could send money back for my children. Then I could go back home.

It was hard. I missed my children. When I finished working on a weekday or had free time on Sunday I would go to the park. Seeing the children playing there and running to the ice cream truck brought me joy because it reminded me of my children and sadness because my children were not with me. Sometimes I would hear the voices of other children and it would sound in my mind like the voices of my children.

When I would get home, I'd see the walls of my room and the top of my dresser filled with pictures of all my children. Sometimes I would sit and watch cartoon shows and wish my children could have been there to see this with me. I almost felt like I was watching the show for them because they couldn't see the cartoon in Jamaica. One day I found a little doll out on the street, and I brought it home with me and put it on my couch so that every day when I came in from work I could see it and remember my children.

My only consolation was knowing I was doing this for them. Although my husband had a farm, he couldn't make enough money to support our family. He'd go to the market, and people would buy his vegetables but then tell him they didn't have the money to pay him. So the checks I sent bought the toilet paper and soap and all the other things my kids needed. And because high school in Jamaica is expensive, the money I made in Canada was the only way my kids were able to get an education.

But every day I spent in Canada I questioned if I was doing the right thing by doing the same thing as my mom.

Three

I was thirty-five when I finally heard from my mother by phone.

"Why didn't you come for me?" was the first question I asked. Her response was she did not have the immigration documentation to come in and out of the country. She could not leave England to get me in Jamaica and then return to her job. I was surprised but touched to hear her call me "Gem," my childhood nickname. But still, I didn't know whether to believe she really loved me. "Do you remember my birthday," I asked? "How could I not remember the birthday of one of my children?" she answered.

I understood. After all, I'd had to leave my own much-loved children. I knew that time and distance could not break the love a mother has for a child.

Once I'd heard from my mother by phone, I talked to her every night after work. Sometimes she sounded sleepy because of the five-hour difference between England and Canada, but I was on cloud nine just to have my mother in my life.

But the distance between us and the realities of our lives as immigrants continued to come between us. We lost contact again for a while after I moved from Canada to the United States. But I tracked her down in 1992 to tell her about the birth of my last son. Then after my mother's phone got disconnected in 1997, I wasn't able to locate her. And when I was finally able to call my mother after getting her number from a cousin, I learned that my mom was terminally ill with lung cancer.

Her wish was to see her little girl. The little girl she had left so many years before—me! For so many years I had wondered if my mother had loved the children she had given birth to in England more than she loved me. But now she told me she would travel with a nurse to the United States just to see me.

She was supposed to come at the end of October 2003. She passed away in the middle of October.

Just as my mom had been unable to come to see me when I was a child because of immigration restrictions, I was unable to go to my mother's funeral in England because of immigration issues.

One of my sons went to the funeral to represent me and my family, while I stayed home and grieved alone. I didn't even tell any of my friends that my mother had died because I thought they would say: "What kind of daughter doesn't attend her mother's funeral?"

Four

I've never told anyone this story before, but I'm telling it today to let my children know how much I love them. Everything I've ever done has always been for them—especially the times it didn't look that way.

If you have never had to grow up away from your mother or be away while your children grow up, take a moment to think how lucky you are. As an immigrant, I am grateful for the opportunities I've had to work in Canada and the United States to make a better life for my family. But few people understand how much parents and children suffer in this process.

Sometimes I feel as though my children do not understand why I did what I did. It pains me to think of the sacrifices they had to make, and I don't think they fully understand the sacrifices I had to make. Every day I thought about my children, but because they didn't know that I feel that they are still hurting.

I know how they feel. As a child, I cried in bed at night, wondering if my mother loved me. As a young adult, I felt sad as I watched other people's children around the ice cream truck because I was unable to see my own kids. And as a woman, I grieved alone while others gathered around my mother's coffin.

But although I'm sometimes sad when I think about my mother today, in my heart I feel at peace. During our conversations my mother told me she loved me, and I believed her because I know how much I love all of my children. And like her, I know how much you must love your children to bear the pain of leaving them so they can have a chance at a better life.

THE RIDE

Jacqueline Doiron

Most kids wait for Christmas, some for spring break, and some for the magical time of summer. I wasn't one of those kids. Don't get me wrong, I liked summer, but those are stories for another time. While all my friends dreamed of summer, I dreamed of the crisp air of fall and "The Ride."

I was that weird kid that everyone whispered about. I already kind of knew how it felt to fly as I had fallen out of a third story window at the age of two and a half. I was always "the sick kid." They even tried to tell my parents I was "retarded". But my Uncle Robert was the cool uncle who brought me a *huge* stuffed dog in the hospital and then, in all the years of growing up afterward, he made sure I had other chances to fly.

Every November my mom, my dad, my sister, and I all piled into the car for the hour drive to Uncle Maurice and Aunt Irene's house in New Hampshire for Thanksgiving. Aunt Irene was the *best* cook and made the most delicious food! But while everybody else was waiting for the turkey, I was waiting for Uncle Robert to arrive. All the sounds of the day mingled together while I waited. Then I'd hear a low, deep rumble that shook the house. A shriek of joy and I was out of that kitchen door screaming, "He's here, he's here, he's here!" I can still see my mom's grimace at how loud I was.

There he was, his huge loveable Grizzly Adams body in the front seat of the newest model of Corvette. He even proudly displayed a glass Corvette on his coffee table at home and would gladly engage in a long conversation about cars. And, while everyone else said hi to my cool uncle, I would almost pass out with anticipation waiting. Finally, it was *my* turn! My turn! My turn! Again, the grimace on mom's face. "Jackie calm down," she would say as I bounced in a circle around Uncle Robert. "Jackie! Calm down!" just a little more sternly. And my smooth and handsome uncle would come to my rescue saying: "Simone, *you* calm down. I'm here to see her!" A huge smile would cover my face and I would flush with pride as he would pick me up and squeeze me until I could barely breathe.

After that, eating Thanksgiving dinner always took entirely too long! And during the slow torture of the after chat my uncle and I would both grow restless. Finally, smirking and throwing me a quick wink, Uncle Robert would turn to my mom and say "Hey Simone, do you need any cigarettes? I'm going out to grab a pack. Wanna go with me, Jackie?" "Ready!" I'd answer with a face smushed with joy. Then I'd climb into the front seat, which seemed so big to me yet so little to my big Uncle Robert. Everyone would come out to watch us just pull out of the driveway: that's how cool he was. And for the next thirty minutes he was all mine!

Along with fast cars and smoking and drinking, Uncle Robert loved loud music. I can still remember the Doors "Light My Fire" playing in his car as we roared down the road with the top down. The rumble of the engine and the music would vibrate through my body, and both of us would disappear into the energy of the moment. We would zoom down the road, up the hill, right past that convenience store we'd said we were going to. And Uncle Robert would look at me with his beautiful smirk and say, "We'll grab those cigarettes on the way back." Then he'd pull onto the highway and off we shot like a lightning bolt in a thunderstorm. The wind blowing in my face, my hands in the air. "Eeeeeeeeeeee, faster!" I would shriek as his foot pushed down on the gas pedal! We drove so fast, I imagined I was flying! Sometimes I would see a hawk in the air floating above and imagine we were racing! It was magical! He was magical!

Uncle Robert rarely smiled, but he always smiled as he focused on the road and the dashboard in front of him and kept his hand on the shifter like a movie star in a getaway car in an action movie. When we'd come to the exit, I would think to myself, "He'll slow down this time," but he didn't! He would take that curve like a race car driver, both hands tightly gripping the steering wheel. We would finally only slow down and come to a stop at a light. Then he would turn to me with the widest smile and say, "You can *never* tell your mother about this!" and laugh a big belly laugh! And I, in turn, would pledge, "Never!" "OK then, back home we go," he'd say, and we'd do the very same thing on the way back to the house. Sometimes we wouldn't even get cigarettes and my mom would make him go back out to get her some despite the fact that the convenience store was within walking distance.

Those rides were the best moments of my life.

Later in life I would come to realize those rides were for my uncle as well as for me. So, it wasn't entirely a surprise when my mom called me on a hot August day to tell me Uncle Robert had taken his own life. I think I always knew he had his own demons. An army veteran, he had a long-distance stare in his eyes. Those beautiful steely blue-gray eyes had seen so much. But depression was also part of his family inheritance. He'd only been a teenager when he'd found out about his own father's body hanging from the barbed wire noose he'd used to kill himself.

And I think that's why Uncle Robert understood me, even though we never talked about our demons. Sure, I'd fallen out of a window and was treated as a damaged kid, but I was also sexually assaulted at a very young age and an alcoholic by the time I was a teenager. Then, one after another, I tumbled into abusive relationships in my adult life. It's actually surprising that I'm even here today and can celebrate my twelfth year of sobriety. And that may be thanks in part to my rides with Uncle Robert.

When the two of us would roar out of Uncle Maurice's driveway we were leaving behind the people who wouldn't let us talk about our demons. Unlike everyone else who insisted on just seeing me as another little kid, Uncle Robert really *saw* me and *heard* me. He motivated me to stay alive by expressing myself as exactly who I am. My motto is, "I'm unique . . . just like everyone else!"

As I sit here, I stare at that glass Corvette that was given to me after he passed, and I think of those moments. That glass Corvette has been with me everywhere I've ever lived, and each time I look at it I can feel those rides. And anyone with depression knows how important it is to seize moments of joy. My Uncle Robert knew the power of a fast ride with loud music—and the company of a person who inspires you. And that is how I will always remember my Uncle Robert. Although he finally was overwhelmed by his own demons, he has kept me alive by teaching me to celebrate life every day.

THE CARDINAL RULE

Jamie Thrasher

When you are upset and mad at the world, how do you handle those emotions? Punch a pillow? Go for a walk? For me, the best way to get my emotions out has always been to put them in writing. As soon as I learned how to read and write, I wrote on anything I could. No cardboard box was safe. No wall could stop me. I had to write. I had a story to tell. The written language became the only way for me to tell the truth!

I am a survivor of thirteen years of sexual, physical, mental, and verbal abuse. As a result, for many years I did not have a voice, a say, or a way out. I was forced to stay within my own mind and to take everything in stride and in silence. No one outside the house knew what was going on. My stepfather's cardinal rule was, "What happens in this house, stays in this house." So for my early years I did and said nothing. But this slowly began to change as I learned to read, write, and formulate my own thoughts, and as I gained the power of written language.

Before I could read and write I had a crazy, magnificent, ever-expanding imagination. In the '90s we didn't have smartphones or tablets to calm fussy babies on buses. Instead, my mother always carried a small bag filled with books just for me. As we rode through the city to our destination, I looked at the pictures and imagined myself within the pages, standing with the characters. When the books could no longer hold my attention, I looked out the window and imagined the characters running alongside the bus. An entire conversation with the characters, as they ran alongside, would go through my head. I think these experiences were similar to George Orwell's, who was also a lonely, isolated child. His tendency to make up stories because of his loneliness and need for validation was also a habit I had. I told countless fibs and white lies because those lies were better to come up with than to speak the actual truth.

At the same time, the cardinal rule was never to be broken, and I took this job seriously (maybe too seriously). I hid my abuse behind tall tales of bullies at school and lies about my sister hurting me. Whenever I told these made-up stories, my stepfather would show love and affection—and not the inappropriate kind. Once my childish mind decided this was the only way to get him to love me properly, without touching me, this became my way to ask for love and attention.

My earliest memories of writing are of me carefully scripting my spelling words over and over, five times each until I was able to pass my mother's verbal test, to ensure I would pass that week's spelling test. Then came the always-dreaded book report! I struggled with this as a child, but still my mother pushed. And with time, I gained the skill of retelling a story and putting it into my own words.

When I was in second grade, my mother decided to go back to school herself. Now the tables turned, and soon I was the one giving my mother verbal tests to ensure she knew words, definitions, and spelling. These words were not words an eight-year-old would normally use, but I learned them anyway. People always commented on the way I spoke and how formal I could be. I believe these words have formed the way I have evolved as a writer.

Oddly enough, I also got plenty of practice learning new words and definitions thanks to my stepfather. His second favorite punishment was making me write out the word and definition of every word in the dictionary from A to whenever he felt like letting me stop. This improved my writing skills beyond those of any kid my age by far.

I badly wanted to tell everyone what was going on at home—how hurt, scared, sad, and lonely I felt. But I stuck to my stepfather's cardinal rule. Instead of speaking, I began to write it down anywhere I could. I remember an eight-year-old me walking into my room, my face hot from his beard rubbing on my cheeks, my chest numb and tingling from his touch. I sank to the floor in front of my chalkboard and began to write. I had never in my life written so much, so quickly. As my pain transferred to words I filled a twenty-four by twelve inch chalkboard in a matter of twenty minutes. After turning this moment of abuse into hundreds of words, however, I had to erase every single word. I cried as I wiped away each word, knowing my truth would forever be gone without anyone else seeing it. I was too young and uneducated about mental health to know it yet, but I was using a grounding technique. I was writing every sense I could remember or feel, to make it exit my head and transfer to whatever I was writing on.

I felt the burden of the cardinal rule once more when I was visiting a cousin. My cousin and I were in the basement with my uncle. He was a huge computer nerd, and every inch of the basement was covered in computers, computer parts, and accessories. He had one that was an old-school, gray, bulky dinosaur of a computer. It didn't seem to be powered on, so I started to play with the keyboard, typing randomly. Then my wandering fingers began to type out my story. I typed a few words then erased them. A few more words, then backspace. It became a plus and minus game, trying to keep track of each letter I typed, making sure the backspace was equivalent to or more than what was typed. I held the backspace for a few moments to ensure anything I had written was gone. Then I typed out, "Kenny is molesting me." As I typed this, my uncle turned to look at me. "Oh, that's actually on you know," he said and walked toward me. My heart began to race as I rushed to the backspace button and held it with all my might. He stood beside the stool I was sitting on and pressed the power button to the monitor. The screen turned on and relief overcame me. The words I had written were gone . . . I hadn't broken the cardinal rule.

In middle school my love for language, words, reading, and writing began to bloom. In sixth grade we began to learn different elements and kinds of poetry: alliteration, haiku, and odes. But what sparked my creative mind was "The Tell-Tale Heart," by Edgar Allen Poe. He wrote in a darkness I have never seen anyone else write. I could identify with his language and tone; it was a side of me I knew was in there but had been unable to explore. After reading this story in class I went home that night and went to work. I was inspired! I wrote the darkest, creepiest poem I could about a monster.

When I was done, I was so proud of myself I couldn't wait to share a written piece! I could show off my language, my personality, and my own words. I ran into the living room to show my mother and stepfather. My notebook was in my hands as I read the poem, and then my stepfather became enraged. He grabbed my notebook and ripped it out the whole page. "What the fuck is this! We don't write shit like this! What is your problem?" he yelled as he ripped the page into pieces. He handed it back to me and ordered me to throw it away. I walked away defeated, unheard, and again I followed the cardinal rule. Thinking back, it's funny that my own personal monster was offended by my made-up monster story. I brought reality to the table and he wasn't satisfied with his well-deserved dish.

No matter how many times I tried to speak about anything, my words meant nothing to him, or to my mother. I had written my story multiple times, told myself the story multiple times. I could hear me, the page could hear me, but the world couldn't. However, writing saved my life in a time that would be difficult for anyone, never mind a small child who only knew this life and nothing more. I had no advocate, no support, I was truly alone. My stepfather threatened that my siblings and I would all be separated if I spoke. He even threatened my mother's life when I tried to stand up to him. So instead, I turned to paper and pen and got everything out, the ugly, the mean, the truth, all of it.

When I finished writing until I couldn't anymore, I felt better, but still completely unheard. As George Orwell wrote: "Writing a book is a horrible, exhausting struggle, like a long bout of some painful illness. One would never undertake such a thing, if one were not driven on by some demon whom one can neither resist nor understand." What better way to describe my drive that day . . . I, a Catholic (honest to god) believer, can tell you, I saw the devil in his eye that day. That demonic action caused my hands to write as if bewitched. When I was finally finished and let all of my emotions out on that blackboard I felt exhausted, depleted, and still lonely as ever. The demon never left after I wrote, no matter how much *better* I felt after writing. That remaining demon is what kept me writing for many years to come.

I did speak my truth to a few cousins my own age, but they couldn't understand the gravity of my situation. And neither could I. But even this action flirted with breaking the cardinal rule, and I was just not brave enough to completely cross that line yet. As I got older, though, I understood the situation better, and I was growing old enough to know that if I spoke again, they would believe me. However, I wasn't ready for the consequences of my words. I didn't want to lose my stepfather; he was the only father I had. And I had yet to see how I had been completely manipulated.

This all changed when I was sixteen years old. My cousin Cassandra came to ask me about something I had told her as a child. I was taken aback that she remembered. I couldn't even attempt to lie. My face said everything she needed to know. A few months later, cops were surrounding my house and arresting my stepfather. Six months after his arrest, we were sitting on the benches of the Springfield Courthouse, awaiting his trial. Our turn came and the room was emptied for my and my sister's privacy.

When I was called forward, I held in my hands two pages. These pages were a record of thirteen years of abuse and torment, summarized in a polished and painfully true five-paragraph essay. The first draft of that statement was five pages long, filled with everything he had ever done to me and my sister. But due to the way the law worked, I had to remove some of the claims I made because they were not what I had said in the original police statement. This record, although short and sweet, gave me the strength and power, finally, to do what needed to be done for so many years! Due to my testimony and his guilty plea, he was sentenced to thirteen years at a jail in Gardner, Massachusetts. I was beyond happy; finally, after all these years, I was free, all because of everything I had learned about language and writing and expressing myself. Speaking my own words for once, breaking the cardinal rule and having my truth heard, was more vindicating than anything.

I hope my ability to understand language and its many applications will help me continue to make something out of myself. I hope my words will find the ears that need to hear. I hope my language saves another whose background matches mine. I hope that through my words others will find comfort in the fact that they are not alone and that someone else out there completely understands them. I hope my testimony saves a life, or ends a situation of abuse because I educated them. My journey with language has been a long one but I will never again be silenced!

DANGER

ARE YOU A PRODUCT OF YOUR ENVIRONMENT?
OR ARE YOU A PRODUCT OF YOUR CHOICES?

Jess Rivera

Hey yo, this personal narrative is dedicated to my food stamp getting, public housing living, foreign car dreaming, foster home hopping, bottom of the totem pole goal gettas. Regardless of your financial situation, or your current circumstances, I want to encourage you to make a plan to intentionally keep getting it out of the mud. Whether you are reading this in the United States or across the globe, I've opened up in hopes to inspire you to get over your adversity, to be persistent. May you continue becoming a better version of yourself and make your journey toward progress worth it.

I have realized no one is coming to "save me." And for that reason, I have taken accountability and full responsibility for my life and how I navigate it. Don't get it twisted. I don't turn down help, nor am I too proud to ask for it when I need it. But I've learned one thing for sure—when you give over the power to feed you, you give others the power to starve you. And from my personal experiences, relying or depending on others exposed me to shark-infested waters. Despite the programs out there providing you with resources, financial assistance, or a place to call home, becoming self-sufficient and savvy is essential for your independent success. You have the power to minimize the possibility that you fall through the cracks and become another victim or another statistic in the system. Let's get right into it.

Let me give you the game on where it all began for me. I grew up calling the hood, the projects, South Boogie, Hollywood, Dead City, "home." My child-hood and adolescent years were rough as fuck. But it wasn't because of my home structure. I was raised in the projects by a beautiful single Puerto Rican mom with three girls. Growing up in Springfield Housing Authority (SHA) also known as "Dead End Projects" or "Marble St. Housing" came with many challenges—gritty experiences and high exposure to violence.

But living on the third floor with my sisters, in our three-bedroom apartment, was like living in luxurious condos. Mom always had the house laced up with the nicest furniture (in hindsight maybe chairs and sofas remained in mint condition because she wouldn't let us sit on them). Artwork and figurines decorated rooms like you would see in the pages of a home improvement magazine. The floor stayed waxed like that of a high-end executive office, and our rooms were decorated with popular cartoon themes, with sheets and curtains to match.

On the weekends, my mom had a routine. When my sisters and I heard the salsa, merengue, or colta vena (Spanish for slow love songs) playing through these two, four foot high speakers, we knew it was cleaning time and we did not interfere. If we wanted something, we waited. As we tried to be patient, we would clean up our own rooms, entertain ourselves, and watch TV until she was done. She would take forever, I mean seriously, she would start early at like 8 a.m. and be at it for hours. We'd watch Nickelodeon, Cartoon Network, play Mario on the Nintendo, make art with the Light Brite. Do you remember this toy? It had black colored sheets with templates. You'd put them on a board with a light behind it, follow the template design, lightly press little pegs into the template; then it would light up to show you what character you made. It was a hot commodity at that time. Anyway, we would eventually tire ourselves out from keeping busy, which inevitably led us to take naps. Can you believe my mom would still be cleaning at noon?

Oh man, sometimes . . . actually, now that I think of it, she always cleaned the nasty-ass hallways, too. The staircases were filthy, so she would use a separate broom and mop to clean the front and back stairs, which took her even longer. No matter how impatient we got, we knew to leave her be. We did not interrupt or rush her. The collective smell of Fabuloso and Mr. Clean after she mopped was the cue that she was almost done. I have to admit her deep intricate cleaning routine set a high standard for me. It just made everything feel better.

Funny how my sisters and I could sleep all through the loud music my mom blared through those speakers. Even her loud singing couldn't wake us. All that combined with the downstairs neighbors, Jamaican reggae bumping through the walls, the next-door neighbor screaming at her kids on the top of her lungs, and all the commotion going on outside did not faze us. This cacophony was normal in the projects. But something about the great smell of cleanliness and fresh air coming through the windows always woke one of us up. It set the tone for excitement as we knew we'd be doing something fun once my mom was done. Once my sisters or I woke up, we would get bored and wake everyone else. When my mom was finished with her routine we would get all showered up and dressed for the day, to spend quality time with our family or friends or head out of town for adventures.

During the week, mom always had dinner ready for us. When I got home from school with my sisters, we would pop open the security door down-stairs (because the buzzers or doorbells never worked); it was the only way to get into the building. No matter how many women would be cooking in the building, I could tell my mom's cooking apart from theirs. Mind you, we had to go past five apartments before getting to ours. As soon as I opened those heavy hideous blue security doors, I could smell the Jamaican patties from one neighbor, the burnt rice from another. But I knew the smell of my mom's cooking. Mmmmm. My favorite meal was yellow rice with green gandules and seasoned, golden brown pork chops fresh off the stove. I don't know if it was the fresh sofrito my grandmother always sent from Puerto Rico, but I knew Mom's cooking anywhere. I realize now why she cooked for all the parties and holidays. To be real, my mom did a great job of providing for us so you couldn't tell me we lived below the poverty line. How? I didn't know anyone who was coming home to a clean house, a home-cooked meal, and a beautiful loving mom, who would slap some act right into us if she had to.

So, if that was the environment in my household, how could anything be wrong with my upbringing? Despite what the social scientists said about bro-ken families and single moms, my home life and family were inspiring and uplifting. But let me clarify for you where the plot begins to thicken.

Growing up in public housing, you had a variety of different people living in this crowded box-like, dead-end street. You had three buildings to the left and three more to the right, with the road in the middle. These two huge blue dumpsters that overflowed with trash daily were located in between the buildings at the end of the streets, just before the woods. The parking lot was always full of trash, bottles, hazards, plastic bags, cigarette butts, Dutch guts, tape from cassettes wrapped around the poles, and broken CDs that someone tossed out because they were probably too scratched up. The parking lot was dull and rarely clean or safe to play in. The nearby park was flooded with homeless people and addicts—so that was off limits.

Imagine what graffiti-filled hallways looked like or the gross smells that came from some apartments where people did not clean with the same intensity as my mom did? Whatever you imagine it's probably a little worse than that. The stairs would have needles that addicts would leave behind. Little colorful bags emptied of their addictive substances would also be left behind. Blood smeared on the walls from the junkies' veins bursting made the hallways and stairwells look like murder scenes. Piss in the corner of the floor seeping into the wood beneath the tiles and all types of nasty shit surrounded our little oasis. This is probably why my mom did not allow shoes in the house.

You would see raccoons and homeless people constantly going through the trash. The "repurposed units," as I'll refer to them here, were the stuff that homeless people frequently took out of the dumpsters: dressers, reusable metals, and other big items, whatever they considered valuable, filled their shopping carts. They would later clean, polish, and sell the items to pawn shops or they would trade them in to the hustlers (drug dealers) for their fix. Next, there were the "recyclers," who literally had shifts. I can't tell you if it was intentional or not, but they respected each other's routes and schedules. They were very organized. All they did was open trash bags and collect the recyclable cans and bottles. They would take the cans and bottles down the street to a redemption center in exchange for the five-cent recycling deposit that happened to be right next to the liquor store. SHA didn't have a recycling program, so no one who lived in the projects recycled. The dumpsters on our street were a gold mine for others in desperate need. Especially after a long weekend, the trash had more beer bottles than it normally would during the week and was a profitable hunting ground. In my opinion, the trash heaps were a major eye sore, and forcing people to scrounge through them to survive was truly inhumane.

Upon entering the dead-end street into our projects you would also see those who didn't pay much for rent and spent most of their day outside. I'll call them our "community watch." They would be stationed at the end of the projects by the dumpsters from sunup to sundown. My sisters and I would leave for school in the morning, and we would see the same women congregating at the corner every day, with their lawn chairs, like clockwork. After school, my sisters and I would walk home from the bus stop and see the same ladies joined by more women. After 3 p.m., I would notice the group get larger with more people and all the kids playing outside. Don't get me wrong, these ladies were cool. They always greeted us and watched all the kids in the area play outside since it was not safe to play out there without supervision. They kept an eye on the kids. That's how they showed their nurturing side, by looking out for us. If we swore or were caught acting up, they would tell our moms. Some of these ladies were the mothers of our friends, while some would be just "visitors." My mom hung out with them from time to time, but my mom was always grinding (working) so it would be rare. As you can imagine, these women knew everyone's business. They knew who was being served papers for eviction; they knew who was cheating on their man while he was at work; they knew who lived there undocumented; they knew who was working more hours than they reported. Shit, now that I think of it, they had all the tea (gossip). They knew everyone's business, so you wouldn't want any problems with them. Otherwise they'd air out your dirty laundry.

Most days as we headed right out of our apartment door to go to the bus stop in the morning, we would encounter people sleeping on the hallway floor. We would have to excuse ourselves as we walked over these unknown strangers who, unfortunately, became familiar faces over time. I remember opening the door and seeing them hanging out in the hallway, smoking and drinking, with no regard for anyone or their kids. And in case you were wondering why no one called the authorities, if you are from where I'm from, you don't call the police. THAT IS A BIG NO-NO!

I recall these guys who were staying in the apartment with the family next to ours. Turned out they were wanted by police for allegedly murdering a clerk at a liquor store. A few days later, the police rushed into our apartment screaming, "Where are they?" I'm talking about a mob of agents everywhere looking through every room, yelling, swearing, "Where the fuck are they?" with their weapons inches from my face, I was so confused and angry because they were in the wrong apartment. They had the audacity to use the space from our apartment to better position themselves to rush into the apartment next door with no regard for how their mistakes just impacted my family. How would you feel waking up at the crack of dawn to this type of madness? They found their suspects in the apartment next door, and sadly the Department of Child and Family Services took the young kids from our neighbor. The mother lost her kids because she was harboring criminals in her apartment. She eventually also lost her housing benefits and was evicted. I didn't understand the purpose of the ugly heavy-ass security doors. It clearly wasn't keeping anything or anyone hazardous out of our homes or stairwells. They were pointless. Maybe they were trying to keep us in?

One thing is for sure, privacy was a higher luxury. The maintenance crew were not the only ones who had access to enter our home. I can recall many employees had the master key to every apartment unit. This was unsettling because there were always new employees on the premises, and we could not keep up with the changes. SHA employees also had the "discretion" of legally entering any dwelling as they deemed fit. That was an unsettling feeling for me and my family. Seriously, "at their discretion?" With so many new faces, trust wasn't easily given.

Imagine sleeping, attempting to regroup after a rough day, and you are woken up by not one but two "high-class" women with their fancy dresses, clipboards, polished jewelry, in your bedroom! They would announce themselves as you were asleep, three rooms and down the hall, too late because now they've realized someone is knocked out from exhaustion. To my startling surprise, I reacted instinctively, and I became aggressive. I mean, who wouldn't? I'm at my most vulnerable state, deep asleep, and I'm woken up by loud heels, chattering voices, no advance notice, and no regard for the place I call "home." Beyond being confused, to me, they were intruders! Did it make it OK to enter my home without notice? Why? Because they were recently titled the new property managers? Did this give them free range to violate my rights? What did they expect? I had no idea what they looked like, let alone expect them to be in my home, conducting business as usual in their new roles as if this was OK. Plus, hello, they had their nasty shoes in the house! The entitlement was real. I could not help but wonder how the rest of the public housing authority was being managed and what other levels of disregard for tenants was taking place.

This SHA location was home to about forty families "legally"—meaning they were on the lease and had permission to live there. The others were "long-term visitors": boyfriends, fathers, and other people who stayed in the apartments without being on the lease. Some were illegally staying there because they had been convicted of a crime and would not be allowed to legally reside on the property. Others were not allowed to get help or services for reasons like having a case with "pending charges." So much for being innocent until proven guilty.

SHA was income based. This meant that one household could pay twenty dollars for rent a month if you didn't work. Those who worked, like my mom, paid much more, but rent did not exceed more than $525. The rent categories created a bit of a divide in the projects between those who were employed and those who were not. SHA did constant monitoring for an increase in tenants' income. The lease required you to constantly update your income information and household members. It often frustrated my mom and the neighbors. I remember when it was time to renew your lease because I would hear the tenants complaining. Their frustrations were reasonable. They worried about paying rent and paying for college. If every time I make more they take more why work so hard? I would always be ear hustling and could hear their cries and concerns. The SHA monitored tenants' wages like the CIA watched drug cartels. As soon as you made more money from working more, your rent went up. Before you could update SHA, they had already sent you a notice that you needed to provide copies of your pay stubs. Like most government assistance programs that provide services, they wanted to know everything, not to assist you better but to adjust your benefits accordingly. They expected a letter with information from your employer about how long you've been working this job or how often the overtime was going to be available. These dynamics were real disincentives for tenants to work harder. Getting assistance from public housing came with a whole lot of bullshit. However, higher rents did not mean better living conditions. The quality of living did not improve. Paying more did not mean better services.

SHA had to have a high turnover rate for their maintenance workers because there was always a new face with an SHA uniform shirt on. At one point they must have partnered up with the Hamden Sheriff's Department because I would see some of the prerelease guys come around and clean up the premises as community service. Someone had to do it because SHA maintenance workers did not do it, with the exception of one young Puerto Rican maintenance man. I remember this one young Puerto Rican guy who overperformed his maintenance duties above anyone's expectations. He was on top of things. He was committed and didn't come to do a half-ass his job. I think he had a little of my mom in him. He might also have been attracted to her because he was always giving her free paint for upkeep and fixing a chipped floor, and he made it his priority to provide or fix what she needed without her having to call the main office and wait. I'm not sure if he did this for every tenant, but we appreciated it. With his help, my mom always received compliments for having the nicest apartment in the projects. Seriously, she constantly received compliments from the neighbors or whoever would come to our home. He was an outstanding maintenance man, regardless of his motives.

But all the other maintenance guys, they underperformed. This went on for so long that I can't help but assume they were allowed to slack off on the job. You would not see one maintenance worker for hours. You would have to go to the maintenance basement, which was in the community room, and it was like their hangout. The one Puerto Rican maintenance guy who I rarely saw slacking later showed me the man cave they had set up because I was so curious about where they would spend their shifts. They were very comfortable down there. Nice big TV, fridge, Sega game, a basketball hoop, I mean, they had the works, and it was a perfect setup for slackers. It must've been nice to go to work and get paid to do nothing work related. I knew when their supervisors were around on the premises because they would suddenly be seen doing their jobs, scattering like cockroaches when the lights come on. The sound of leaf blowers was heard; sweeping was seen; the outside trash was finally picked up; the stairs were mopped for the first time in forever. Maybe the inside of the building smelled more because they never did their job or perhaps even worse after they used the dirty, nasty, moldy old mops when they did do their job. It was bad, seriously, they did the worst job ever. It was ridiculous.

As I grew older, I started wondering how this situation was allowed to occur and why. The Mickey Mouse maintenance work that I witnessed being done on the property truly didn't make sense to me. How could they just paint over the blood on the walls? That's a major health concern, isn't it? There had to be protocols to follow to safely sanitize the apartments and hallways, right? Who knows! All I know is when a family moved out, a new family moved in within days. Shouldn't maintenance sanitize and deep clean? Instead, they did the same lazy-ass job prepping the apartment for the next family to quickly move them in. I'm talking about in a matter of days someone was already pulling up in a moving truck unpacking their belongings. Since SHA employees didn't live there, you could clearly tell by their lack of effort that they didn't care. Eventually, as I would become friends with some of the newcomers, I'd get to see how their homes differed from my home. And that shit looked crazy. But I guess it beats being in the streets or in a shelter. It's as if SHA employees expected folks to settle for whatever they got. The tub was the one thing that stood out to me once because it looked brown and rusted. There's no way the new family that just moved in caused that much wear and tear like that. The edges had mold—like damn straight-up disregard for people and their well being. I also recall the knobs to the sinks having food particles in the crevices. It was just gross. Don't even get me started on what they did on extermination days.

The things I was exposed to and witnessed as soon as the brown doors to my home closed behind me were ruthless. I was not the only one experiencing this lifestyle though. With so many other kids in the area and their single mothers living in this cell-like jail structure with one way in and one way out, it was traumatic. The way we were living and the things we were exposed to is what you would mostly see in R-rated movies or on Cops TV.

SHA is supposed to be an organization developed to assist low-income families with a place to live. But was that it? Create a well-written mission and vision statement, get the funding, and pretend everything is running smoothly, even though it wasn't? Where was the follow-up, where were the people in charge, the higher-ups? There were so many issues, so many unanswered questions and yet no improvements to increase the quality of life in our neighborhood.

As I got older I began to research the SHA mission and what could be done to build a better community. With very little encouragement and access to information, I began to notice there was a major misalignment of SHA's program goals and its tenants' experiences. SHA documents all seemed like lies—fabricated well-written bullshit. I did not see how anyone believed SHA was helping us. The claim that they "are dedicated to providing a well managed, well maintained and high-quality housing" was far-fetched. Their attention was supposed to focus on "build[ing] communities and neighborhoods which promote self-sufficiency." Seriously? How? Maybe I was reading the wrong SHA mission and vision statement, but this was not my experience. My personal experience living on SHA property was beyond alarming.

How was all of this allowed? Where do you turn to just to ask questions, let alone get answers? What do you do when you need to express your concerns without fear that someone in power would retaliate? Many of us who lived here were black/Jamaican or Puerto Rican—there were a few Jewish and Irish people. The frustration grew into animalistic instincts for survival in some of us.

Living in the hood was no walk in the park. These can't be the political issues being discussed because, if so, the politicians were failing us big time. Where was the disconnect? How can these people say they are helping, yet all I see are struggling families, drug-infested hallways, and a system built to "help" letting many mothers and their children down. So I sincerely sympathize with the many who are currently being raised in these failed, structured systems, near and far.

Springfield Housing Authority was the organization that provided income-based housing for my family for almost nineteen years. In my highly informed experience, I have concluded they were really comfortable simply being slumlords. And no one challenged these conditions. If what I have described doesn't vividly paint the picture of my environment, let me just sum it up: it is nothing like these politicians, housing representatives, and community leaders describe. SHA has a "mission," but their statement and their "vision" did not reflect what I was experiencing in real time. My real-life experiences and their program's mission did not correlate.

I confidently believe that my environment and experiences were the reason I scored high on the ACES test (a study that measures childhood experiences and the correlation between chronic illnesses and other concerns). We had very limited resources while living there. Although my mom did an amazing job to shelter us from the reality of what was happening around us, her efforts stood no chance against the systemic issues of poverty. I have no recollection of anyone making it out of the projects to become property owners or achieve anything major. Unless you want to call high-profile drug dealers and prostitution a success. We didn't see many happy endings. I'm not sure what SHA was really aiming to accomplish as an organization, but the options for us in that place were very limited and did not reflect their so-called desired goals. My experiences were not just extreme exposure to traumatic events; I'd call many of these experiences major civil rights violations, which took place openly on SHA premises.

My environment didn't give me many choices; therefore, the limited access didn't provide many luxuries for me. I had to work with what I had. Without much guidance, I quickly learned from my environment and picked up some bad habits. I became a product of that environment. The environment taught me survival; it taught me I had no place in the world outside the projects. I learned that going to jail or dying young was what awaited all of us who came from here. That's what SHA exposed me to. Although SHA isn't to blame directly or entirely, I believe the environment they fostered was the opposite of what they claimed in their vision statement, ultimately failing many of us. Therefore, I feel the neglect was so deep-rooted and overlooked that it resulted in me becoming a victim of their flawed system. Through them I learned policies and politics come before people.

Unfortunately, after much political talk over the years, Massachusetts voted in favor of the MGM casino in 2016. Was it a coincidence that around the same time SHA was starting to get more involved, by conducting inspections in the apartments they had neglected over the years. I'm talking about these inspections occurring more frequently. They went from once a year, if that, to about four to six inspections a year, depending on the conditions of the apartment. I saw the politicians around the neighborhoods with their long fancy overcoats and leather gloves, and I remember thinking to myself, huh, they're finally about to clean things up around here. Unbeknownst to me, I started to also hear more talk about the casino being built on Main Street, which was too close for comfort. But with so much speculation and not enough accurate facts, I disregarded the topic.

Living in the SHA projects for so long, I saw how the politics played out. I sat and waited for a long time to see how the casino's proposal came to be. While dates and times for political discussion may have been accessible to the public, I can't help but wonder where they posted the public notices of information. Was it intentionally only available during hours of operation in a locked room with limited access that only SHA had keys to? Of course, with little pushback from the people everything worked in favor of the casino. Sadly, many of the families living in SHA were displaced, the voucher that was promised never made it to many of us, and I wonder what came of the forty-six-plus families that were growing up in those projects. In 2018 the buildings were knocked down, and the dead-end street is now a public road that many drive through without the slightest idea of what it had once bred.

We are in desperate need of structural change. I recognize that no system is perfect, but we can't continue to see the statistics and be selectively and willfully blind. Victims are falling through the cracks of these systems, which are supposedly put into place to improve lives and assist anyone in need. Don't forget how your decisions impact the lives of us, the oppressed. The quality of our lives should reflect these promises, not the little effort and resources put into realizing them. We deserve people in power who aren't selective about what they share or implement. Whatever you are in alignment with and whichever organization you are collaborating with, the aim should be to serve people with respect and dignity. The results of the missions and visions should reflect the people's experiences. I ask you who read this to be in alignment with your heart's true calling. Find a cause your heart can commit to and remain consistent. If you work for public housing, even if temporarily, please make your greatest effort to uplift those you serve by providing excellent service, especially maintenance crews.

As people in power begin to step into positions or rise up in the ranks, I truly hope they stick to core fundamental morals and values that respect, encourage, and empower those they serve. I hope they stand for things that are for the greater good and put people before profits. I hope they are living intentionally to improve our quality of life. If you are a teacher, teach your heart out, be a resource. Keep listening to learn. Apply the information provided in your training and pass down that knowledge. If you serve, serve wholeheartedly to those who may never be able to repay you. If you manage a property or a team, lead with excellence and contribute to your followers so they can accurately represent and have a role model they can follow. I'm calling the real leaders to rise and lead from the front. Be an upstander! Your actions in these positions of power are the voices for the voiceless. Society is molded by your vision; don't just pretend to inspire hope with empty promises to get you recognized in public—only to fail us in private. Put action behind your words, it's time to *walk that walk*. Let's do better. Anyone can look good; it's time to *be* good.

I couldn't accept how long the wool was pulled over my eyes. I refuse to become another statistic. I began making healthier choices and went back to school to empower my people. I am tired of attending funerals and jails more than weddings or graduations. This was normal growing up, but this has to change. I realize I can't wait until things impact me directly to learn more about an issue. If I wait to care or get involved until something negatively impacts me, my opponents have a head start and I am doing myself a disservice. I advocate against being ignorant or remaining arrogant. Ignorance is not bliss; it will most likely make you a casualty of profits. I became aware of my constitutional rights. When you come from the hood, those who work in these areas maximize and prey on your lack of knowledge and you become a target. Meanwhile they receive recognition for a "job well done," even if they've negatively impacted your life. Understanding your rights is essential to living a fulfilled life. Set the standard, so you can be treated respectfully, fairly, and justly. Thankfully this is part of my come-up story. What's yours?

To be continued . . .

LESSONS LEARNED

Debra Francis

When I was only twenty years old, I had a four-year-old daughter and I was pregnant again. And I was homeless.

My partner, Kendall, had just built a five-bedroom house back home in Trinidad—a friend had given him the land. When the home was built, the man asked to move in with us. Six months later he asked us to leave. He said, "Break the house down," and so we had to break it down. The house had cost us a lot of money, and now we had to move out.

I had nowhere to go. I couldn't go to my parents' two-bedroom house because it was full with my brother and other siblings. So I ended up on the street.

Kendall kept asking around until he found a gardener who would let us stay in his toolshed until the baby was born. The toolshed was made of galvanized metal. Since there were no windows, there was no place for the heat to go. Life was so humid and stressful that I worried I'd get a stroke while I was pregnant.

To make the shed into a temporary home, Kendall spread empty chickpea sacks on the dirt floor and made a torch soaked in kerosene to provide light. I cooked on a sheet of metal propped up by three big stones over a fire. The only dishes we had were calabash gourds, and we'd eat out of them with our hands. There was no water, so I would get up each morning and walk to the spring a mile away to bathe and wash clothes. Then I'd wait until the sun went down when it was cooler to walk home.

One Sunday morning I was alone with my four-year-old daughter in the shed when the pains started. I sent my little girl to find a neighbor to help.

When I got to the hospital and heard the doctors order a C-section, I began to connect myself in prayers to God. But I had just started to call on God when I heard the first cries of my son, Jelani. He may have been born when we were in poor circumstances, but his name means "mighty." Soon afterward I returned to the toolshed. My daughter, Alana, had to start sleeping on the dirt floor so I could keep baby Jelani with me on the makeshift bed Kendall put together out of a tree trunk. I kept praying to the Lord to send us someone sensible to lend us a helping hand and to give me the strength to bear these difficulties.

We finally moved into our brand new three-bedroom home on Mother's Day, just two months before Jelani's first birthday. I put my daughter in kindergarten and my son in a nursery while I earned a degree in practical nursing and began my career in nursing homes and private hospitals.

While working as a nurse, I also went into the business of selling "doubles," a Trinidadian treat. The whole family would help. Each day when I'd get home from helping my patients, I would wash all the pots and pans. I'd knead the dough for the next day's doubles at 10 p.m., and then my husband and I would get up at one o'clock to roll and fry the flat breads. When Jelani was in primary school, he'd get up at three to put the channa (chickpeas) on to soak. By six my husband would be on the road selling doubles out of an icebox on his bike. In the morning, he would sell doubles to people looking for breakfast. Later in the day, he'd sell to people coming home from work. By that time, Alana was home from school and already cooking the chickpeas for our next day's doubles: fried flat breads, curried chickpeas, and all the sauces: tamarind, pepper, mango, and golden apple. They were the best doubles in Western Trinidad. Business was good.

Thanks to good luck and the hard work of the whole family, by the time my second son was born he had his own crib, his own bedroom, and hot and cold running water. And I'm happy that my second daughter, Shanika, never had to know what it was like to live in a toolshed.

But I have learned a lot from my journey, and so have my husband and children. We know what it's like to be homeless. And we know not to judge people who need the help of others. Today, my husband—who is still back in Trinidad—helps people renovate their homes for free. Jelani gives books and groceries and other supplies to children and the elderly in Trinidad. Alana helps children and churches in need both here and in Trinidad. And I am always ready to speak up for those who need an advocate, and to raise money for the things my community needs: lights, drains, trash pickup, or anything else. I've even given a lot to people in Trinidad who needed to build homes. In fact, the person who made us break down our first home eventually became a vagrant, and I helped him.

Back when I was living in the gardener's shed, I used to call on God to give me the strength to bear my burdens and to send us someone to lend a helping hand. Being poor, hungry, and homeless—especially with small children—is a sad thing. That's why I am grateful today to be able to give back to others and to remind them that with God all things are possible.

VOICELESS

Judy Gustafson

Monday

5 a.m.

I wake up because my heart is pounding, it feels like it's beating against my rib cage. I'm taking short, rapid, shallow breaths as though I were running. I woke up so quickly that I'm still a little disoriented. I'm fighting the fog enveloping my brain to understand exactly what danger I am in. It feels like trying to punch my way out of a cloth sack. I vaguely remember that I felt my car move. I rapidly scan the parking area to see what is happening. It's nothing. Someone parked too close to my car and bumped their door against mine. I take long, slow, deep breaths to calm myself. There's sweat on my skin from my panic, but the frigid January air outside the car has seeped in so I feel clammy. I take off my blanket and turn on the engine for heat. I'm cold enough to justify wasting the gas.

The back seat would be much more comfortable; it's softer and I could curl up with my head on a pillow. But I've watched people break into cars and I know it takes only seconds. If I'm sound asleep on the back seat and someone breaks in, the car could be driving down the highway before I wake up enough to realize what is happening. A woman in a moving car is called "bought and paid for." So I sleep in the driver's seat with my keys near my right hand and my cell phone in my bra. I pray that if someone considers stealing my car while I'm sleeping, they'd be put off knowing that they'd have to move me out of the driver's seat before they could pull away.

5:30 a.m.

There's no more sleep for me today, but I'm calmer and not cold anymore. I turn off my car and wander into the twenty-four-hour retail chain store to use their public restroom and stay safe and warm without burning gas. I like parking in their lot, but I'm careful not to do it every night; I don't want to attract attention. They have the reputation for being very friendly to campers and others who sleep in vehicles, but every location is different because store-level managers may not approve of that company policy. Not all parking lots are safe. I'm trusting a judgment call with crossed fingers each time I stop for the night, but this location has been good so far.

6:00 a.m.

Back in my car. I don't want to stay in the store too long. If I'm asked to leave, I'll have to find another spot to stay at night. I eat a granola bar and an apple that I bought in the store. I try to purchase what I need from the places I stop for the night so no one can say that I'm not a customer. After I eat, I browse through my cell phone, catching up with social media and the news, killing time until my next location opens. I don't want to linger long enough to be noticed.

7:00 a.m.

I leave the lot and drive to the gym about two miles away. The fitness center I belong to has a ten-dollar monthly membership. I shove a clean change of clothes into my gym bag and walk in. They've just opened. I work out for a while and then use their shower. I sometimes wonder if the staff notices that I shower and change there daily, but if they do, they don't mention it. I try not to interact with them; I don't want them to remember me even though I'm probably not the only one using their facilities this way. I'm grateful to have somewhere to shower. I know people who don't have that luxury. My heart breaks for them, but I don't take them with me. The gym itself is average; the equipment is nothing to write home about. It doesn't compare well to other fitness centers that I've belonged to in better times, but my self-esteem is already in the gutter. I am afraid of how I will feel if I can't

figure out a way to bathe daily, so I'm fiercely protective of my membership;
I can't risk losing it.

7:45 a.m.

I leave the gym feeling better and drive to the church where I volunteer,
about thirty minutes away. I am very, very careful to separate my church and
volunteer work from the communities where I sleep. I haven't told anyone
I volunteer with that I'm homeless. During the day I'm an advocate. On
paper, a homeless person advocating for other homeless people makes a great
story. In reality, I find that I have a terrible need to have one area of my life in
which people see me as "normal" and I know that I contribute to the world.
If I broke down and admitted what my life was like, I am certain that my
church community wouldn't love me any less. They would support me and
comfort me. Being honest would help me to help others because we could
identify with each other. But I used to be a professional. I can find support
and comfort elsewhere; my work is the only place I have purpose, the only
place I feel like I used to, competent and assured. So I smile and wear a mask
out of desperation.

9:00 a.m.

I'm in my office; I hear loud voices in the driveway. I grab my cell phone and
church keys and run outside. I don't see my pastor on my way out the door,
and, judging by what I just heard, I don't have time to look for him. Eddy is
standing in the church driveway, telling another one of our flock to put up
his fists. The other guy looks scared. I take a deep breath and step in between
them. It's something I'm cautious about doing. All my attention is fixed on
Eddy, who I'm facing. But I feel other community members gather close.
Someone tries to pull me away. I turn my head, look in their eyes, and say
"NO!" Then snap my attention back to Eddy. He looks a little surprised. He
has reason to be. I'm female. I'm half his height, and I'm clearly out of shape.
As an ex-boxer he could kill me before I could land a punch.

I look in his eyes to hold his attention. I say as calmly and quietly as I can,
"This is church property, you can't do this. What you do elsewhere is your
business, but fighting isn't allowed here." It feels like everyone around me
(myself included) is holding their breath. There's complete silence for a few

seconds. Then Eddy inhales deeply and starts yelling. He doesn't restrict himself to shouting—his arms flail around, his feet stomp, and spit flies out of his mouth (though not in my direction). I feel the guy behind me slink away. I want him to. I've been thinking intensely "walk off, walk off," as though the thought could transfer without sound from my brain to his. I'm wondering what took him so long. I stand there watching Eddy, waiting for him to quiet down enough to hear me. Strangely, I'm not afraid. In the middle of all the drama I have no fear that he will hurt me, although logically I should be terrified. He eventually runs out of breath, and I start to talk to him, repeating some of what he's just said to show I've been listening. His eyes widen and his face relaxes, just a little.

We end up having a conversation. Most people wouldn't do what I've just done, but I'm homeless too and I understand that at least half of Eddy's anger comes from frustration. Another quarter probably comes from helplessness, and none of it is directed at me. Eddy is a powerful man who can't solve his problems. In his heart, he feels unmanned, neutered. Hitting someone his size helps a little, and I can understand why. Stepping in between *was* dangerous, but I'm wearing partial armor. Everyone in our mission's city, homeless and housed, knows who we are and what we do, and many of our flock are profoundly grateful. I knew I wasn't safe, but I also knew I was safer than most people would have been.

12:00 p.m.

I take a break and head upstairs to the sanctuary to pray. I'm feeling a little overwhelmed and frustrated by the magnitude of problems I'm trying to help solve. Sometimes I identify so strongly with the people I'm working with that I can almost feel their pain on my skin, like a physical presence. The vast majority of our guests are homeless. Some stay in shelters, some live outside, some couch surf, some live in cars or abandoned buildings or even worse situations. All feel traumatized, most have been violated by the painful loss of the illusory bubble of safety that most of us believe exists around us. Some never had that false security. They are the sex trafficked, abused children, survivors of domestic violence, people who have fled from one unimaginable situation only to tumble into another one. Most have severe mental health issues, sometimes exclusively from trauma (it's said that if you don't have a mental health issue before you come to the street, wait a minute). None of them will ever truly feel that security bubble again because the knowledge that safety is a temporal chimera has been beaten into them.

The homeless are not who I thought they were in my previous life. I've learned firsthand they are not failures—they are doctors, nurses, psychologists, artists, musicians, moms and dads, grandmothers and grandfathers. Many are smart, talented, and funny. They had lives before catastrophe hit, and every single one wants to get back to living that life. Some never will. They will die on the streets dreaming of normalcy. It's so tempting to blame people for the disaster that wrecks them. When I was more secure I know I said things like "if he didn't do drugs, he wouldn't be homeless," "if she was a better daughter, her mother would have let her stay at home." Now I know those statements came from fear and ignorance. Because if the disaster isn't the fault of the homeless person, it can happen to anyone. It happened to me. I kneel and pray for a while, then I sit and enjoy the quiet and solitude. I will eventually go downstairs and dive back in, but it's so nice to just sit in peace and breathe.

3:30 p.m.

I've worked all day feeding and helping other people. I feel like myself. I took some time to use the mission's phones and computer equipment to work on my own situation, and I think maybe I've made a little progress. When I'm at the church I feel safe, happy, and comfortable, but the church closes at 4 p.m., so now I'm thinking about tonight. I've taken food from the kitchen (with the pastor's permission), so I won't have to buy anything for dinner. The pastor knows I'm poor and why—that doesn't bother me. It's homelessness that I think of as shameful. He doesn't think that way; he ministers to homeless people all day long without public or private judgment. I know him well and I know that I can trust him. But somehow homelessness feels like failure, more than poverty.

It's bizarre, it doesn't make sense, but some irrational part of me seems to believe that if I'd tried harder or done things better, I wouldn't have gotten sick, I would have been able to succeed at one of the twenty jobs I tried on my downward slide. I would have figured out something. I understand that it's not rational to think that way, but it doesn't matter. It's what I feel on a visceral level; logic and experience have had absolutely zero impact thus far. I am a passionate advocate for others. I fight, I rail against racism, sexism, ageism, ableism, and more. But somewhere in the depths of my soul, when I think about my own situation only, I'm classist. When I stop to think about myself, a quiet voice inside of me repeats relentlessly, "I don't belong here, I don't deserve this, it's not fair. I had a home, I went to college, I didn't do anything to deserve this, IT'S NOT FAIR." If I think professionally about those statements, I can easily acknowledge that no one deserves to be here, no one belongs here, none of this is fair for anyone. I teach and believe that most Americans are a paycheck or two away from joining me, irrespective of income. But I know where I came from, and there's a little tiny piece of me always screaming in pain. So, I try to think as little as possible about my current life unless I'm actively working on changing it.

4 p.m.

Time to go. I've put it off as long as possible, but I have to slowly get back in my car and drive away until tomorrow. I drive to a little pond that I like about halfway to my sleeping community and park. I read a book, call my daughter, pray, take a walk, and eventually eat my dinner. The entire time I'm trying to pretend that I just happened to stop here on my way home because I like the scenery. No one is watching me, no one cares what I am doing, there's no one here in the middle of a New England winter except me. I'm trying to lie to myself because the thought of my homelessness during these moments is unbearably painful to me. I wonder, is it a transitional thing because I'm leaving the church where I can pretend to be me and heading to the reality of a parking lot?

6 p.m.

I start my car and drive away from my little park. It's January so it's dark, and the lights are coming on in the houses I'm driving past. It hurts to see how warm and homey they look lit up from the inside, to see families sitting down to dinner, talking, watching TV. I am so aware that I am outside looking in. I try to remind myself that someday I will have another home, that I'm driving over a speed bump and I'm not at the end of my journey. I tell myself all the comforting things I say to other people. I know those statements are true, but right now, in this moment, a normal life seems impossibly far away, and I'm sitting in the car that I'll sleep in tonight. When I get to the town where I've decided to stay it's still too early to pick a location, so I go to a mall and walk around.

9 p.m.

I leave the mall and try to figure out the safest place to sleep. I parse through my five or six regular places and come up with what I think is the best option. I can't go to the retail store again; I never stay at the same place two nights in a row. There's a rest area on the highway nearby that's well-lit and well fre-quented by others, with a bathroom and fast-food restaurant that are open all night. It's not my favorite spot but it seems reasonably safe. When I get there, I look for an available space that is more inconspicuous than all the others. I'm always afraid I'll be "found out" and told to leave. I'm not sure why I'm afraid; worse things have happened to me and I'd just drive somewhere else. Maybe it's because it feels like it would be shameful, like whoever told me to go would do it because they knew I wasn't even good enough to take a park-ing space away from a real customer. I'm always teetering on the edge of the chasm of severe depression. I know if I let go and allow myself to fall I won't get out of homelessness for a long time, so I've developed lots of mental tricks to keep my fingers hanging on to the edge. Potential rejection, yet another blow to my self-esteem, terrifies me, and I avoid it as much as possible. I use the restroom, go back to my car, unfold my blankets, lay my seat back, kick off my shoes, and try to get as comfortable as possible. I pull out my phone because I can't run the car battery down by putting on a light to read a book, and anyway, I wouldn't want to attract attention to the fact that I'm a woman sitting in a car alone, all night. I kid myself that I can hide the light of my cell phone with the blanket so no one will know I'm there. I know better, but if I don't have something to focus on I'll obsess about my situation. I won't sleep for a long time, until the parking lot is almost empty. Another long night.

Church—Three Years Later

I'm standing at the back of the church leaning on the wall helping the ushers when the man runs in. He's clearly, visibly upset. He grabs my arm and pulls it, saying "Judy, Judy, you gotta come!" I grab my Narcan out of the drawer of the desk near the wall and run out with him. He hasn't said it's an overdose, but I already see the signs in him and his panic. We go through the front doors and the heat of the day slaps me in the face. As I jog after him, I'm sifting through the faces of the people I've seen that day wondering who it could be. I see a little group in the hardware store parking lot next to the church and as we run over to them, I'm clutching the medicine. I'm not in good shape and by the time I get there I'm already out of breath.

There's a large man sitting in a little blue car with the door open, and people are clustered around him. He's nonresponsive. There's a used needle by his feet, where it fell when his hand went limp. Someone snatches the Narcan out of my hand, rips the package open, shoves it up the man's nostril, and squirts out the medicine. Nothing happens. There's someone in a panic trying to do CPR while the man is sitting upright. I shove him out of the way and tell people to grab the man, take him out of the car, and lay him down, and they do it. I scan my eyes over his body, evaluating his condition. He's tall, he's white, his lips and nails are turning blue, his skin is gray, and he's not breathing. He has no pulse that I can feel. I don't know him, and I feel grateful that he's not one of our flock. I drop to my knees and start doing chest compressions. He's not moving, not responding, but his body temperature is still warm. I don't know how long he's been there.

I yell to one of the bystanders, "Has 911 been called?" and someone calls back, "Yes!" I keep pumping and debate rescue breathing. There don't seem to be any substances or bodily fluids around his nose or his mouth. I don't know what his medical history is, what diseases he may have contracted from using IV drugs, but I'm afraid if I don't start helping him to breathe, he'll die. Someone else jumps in, Narcans him again, and starts breathing with him. I'm relieved. I can feel the sweat pouring down my body, my shoulders hurt, I'm out of breath, and I keep going. Suddenly, his whole body convulses, and I can feel and hear him violently trying to suck air into his lungs. I stop chest compressions to see what happens next and someone misunderstands and, thinking I'm tired, pushes me out of the way and continues the compressions. I can see that he hasn't come back to us yet, but I'm breathing so hard I'm panting so I don't stop the person, though I watch him for a few seconds to make sure he's doing compressions correctly. I'm half the size of the person doing the CPR, but if I tell him he'll move out of respect. I don't complain, I'm exhausted. I slowly stand up and look around.

There's a small crowd of people pushing in to see what is happening and I try to back them up so they don't block the resuscitation. There's a little scuffle between two guys about how the man was taken out of the car, and

I step in between them and try to calm everybody down. We are all drunk on our adrenaline, sky high from stress. A police officer arrives at the scene, a young one. He doesn't do much, just tells us paramedics are coming and stands and watches. He's chewing gum. After far too long the ambulance finally shows up and the EMTs take over. Nobody moves. We all want to find out if he makes it, even though he's not known in the neighborhood. He must have come in just to buy his drugs from one of the local dealers. I walk over to the EMTs, and they ask me the usual questions: how many Narcans did we give, how long has he been out, do I know his name, date of birth, and next-of-kin. I answer as many as I can, and other bystanders try to answer the rest. I see him move; he isn't dead. There's nothing I can do now, and I start to walk away.

There's an EMT standing to the side watching. I don't like his stance and I don't like his attitude, but as I walk by, I say, "Thank you." He responds, "I don't know why we bother, we're gonna be back here three times today for the same guy." For some reason, the comment that I've heard so many times before enrages me, probably because of the stray adrenaline still float- ing around in my veins. I say to him as sweetly as possible, "Gee, I'm sorry, that's really annoying. You know what I call that?" He looks at me in a barely interested way and says, "What?" I say slowly and sarcastically, drawing each word out, "Job security" and turn on my heel and walk away.

I'm tired. I walk slowly back to the church, up the stairs, and through the front door. I pause in the foyer to take some deep breaths and calm down. I want to cry because I'm so touched that they trusted me enough to run to me for help, and because I'm frightened by how little I know. My blouse was so cool and silky in the morning when I put it on, now it's wet and sticking to my skin. I smell sweat, and my nice slacks have dirt and little tears on the knees from kneeling on the pavement. There's a blister on my foot from running in heels. I walk upstairs into the sanctuary, trying not to limp. It's a large room, full of our varied congregation. Some members of the homeless community that surrounds our church are present. They always sit in the back of the church. They're invited weekly to come closer, but they don't feel worthy to sit near the altar. They feel dirty and alien, and they choose to hang together in the pews furthest from the front. Some of them are asleep during the service, curled up like hedgehogs. We openly allow this because the two hours that the service lasts could be the only safety they have during the day and the pew cushions are soft.

There's a little rustle and stir among them as I walk in. They saw me run out because they watch everything, constantly alert for danger, and they knew what was happening. It's easy for them to recognize the signs of an event that occurs more than daily in their community. They don't want to interrupt the service to ask, but I can see them looking and hear them moving restlessly in the seats. As I walk by, I give them a thumbs up to let them know that the person made it, and they settle down again. There will be lots of questions later, but for now they can focus.

I stay in the back of the church with my people, but I look up the center aisle to those who have more "normal" lives. Many of them are in nice suits or nice dresses, all of them have no idea that someone almost died; they are focused on what the pastor is preaching. The pastor sees me come back in and nods at me without pausing or missing a beat. Most of the people in nice clothes would care very much about the man in the car, but the signs of his crisis weren't relevant to their lives. They feel safe and secure in their lives and their pews, calmly listening to the pastor preaching an impassioned speech about salvation and redemption. A small minority wouldn't care about the man in the car. Those people would ask me questions like, "Why did you bother? He's just gonna do it again tomorrow," or "Aren't you afraid you'll catch some disease if you touch him?" forgetting that some of our church leadership came out of that community. I find an empty pew, sink down into it, put my head on my arms on the wooden seat back in front of me, and pray. I pray for our community, I pray for the man who overdosed, I pray for the police and the EMTs, not forgetting to include the gum chewer and the jackass who didn't care. I pray for our church and all its members, and I add prayers of thanksgiving with gratitude that I'm no longer homeless. This is my ministry, this is my community, this is my life and I passionately love what I do.

FACULTY ESSAYS

REFLECTIONS ON TEACHING CHANGE

Ousmane Power-Greene

"Professor, you're not gonna believe it!" my student Rachel announced as I rushed into my US history class two minutes late.

"What's that?" I asked, pulling my laptop from my leather bag and setting it down.

"My daughter's teacher didn't like the paper she wrote on Christopher Columbus—you know, based on what we read in our book?"

There were scattered chuckles, and one "oh, lord" from the other adult students who appeared eager to see the look on my face once I heard the story.

"Really?" I patted my front pants pocket in search of the toggle I needed to connect my laptop to the projector.

"Nope. In fact, she even called me in for a parent-teacher conference about it."

I raised my eyebrows, intrigued. "So, what'd your daughter write?"

Rachel motioned to our book, James Loewen's, *Lies My Teacher Told Me*. "The stuff in there? You know, about Columbus and the genocide of the Native Americans? The teacher asked my daughter to write a paper for Columbus Day. So that's what she did. But the truth, you know?"

Apparently, when Rachel's daughter summarized Loewen's first chapter, which exposed the unsavory truth about Christopher Columbus for this paper, her teacher assumed she had made it all up to get attention. But when Rachel told the teacher her daughter got all of it from Loewen's book, the teacher was stunned.

"But good news, Professor. By the end of the meeting, that teacher asked if she could copy the chapter and give it to the other fourth-grade teachers!"

Someone clapped, then the rest of the class joined in the applause, and Rachel stood and bowed as if she had just performed a magic trick. And, actually, in some ways the turn of events in Rachel's story represents a certain kind of magic—an act that might seem to some as impossible. I'm not sure about you, but I never heard of a teacher so dramatically changing his or her perspective when confronted with a new set of ideas. Miraculous, indeed. Hopeful, too.

During a time when the United States confronts a new "moral panic" over what is taught in schools, Rachel's story epitomizes the reason the Clemente Course in the Humanities has meant so much to me. In fact, my entire career as a community educator, camp director, high school teacher, and college professor has been rooted in my desire to share with my students ideas that challenge the grand narratives that inform so much of how we think about the human experience. I didn't begin teaching—let alone teaching history—to force my students to memorize trivial factoids about this or that president, or to impress them with my catalog of knowledge about the Civil War (or any war, for that matter).

Rather, I teach because I love to share with people what I learn about the decisions people make (despite risking bodily harm) to challenge policies and practices that perpetuate inequality. Humanities courses provide us with indispensable intellectual tools necessary to take us one step closer to making the world a more just and equal place. This passion for justice is what informs my teaching—whether in a classroom, in a park, or on a street corner. For this reason, teaching a Clemente course has been one of the most meaningful experiences of my life. Writing books and articles are meaningful, too. So is teaching college students. But community education geared toward adults who have not had the opportunity to complete their college degree is particularly gratifying because it offers a more direct path to promote an important human right: the right to education. Thus, in my opinion, teaching adults who have, for whatever reason, been denied this right is a moral imperative.

Yet, this does not mean teaching US history to a heterogenous group of adults—some of whom only recently arrived in the United States and have never taken US history—is without its challenges. I learned early on to abandon conventional pedagogical approaches that emphasize "coverage" and focus instead on deep, thoughtful engagement with history that promotes further inquiry beyond the classroom, or even promotes social action. In my course, students read the words of the conquerors and the conquered—the oppressor and the oppressed—readings that encourage them to see events from a multiplicity of vantage points. I then ask them to develop arguments rooted in evidence. I make certain our class activities and discussions open the door to further inquiry instead of forcing them to "master" a series of "facts" that shut out inquiry. My students are also encouraged to explore the history of their own communities by, for example, writing essays about a statue or memorial that they pass every day but know very little about. This type of assignment does two things: First, it allows them to focus their historical lens on something in their community. Second, it provides them with an opportunity to think critically about the way historical markers represent an uncritical, often exaggerated or romanticized, view of people or events in the past.

Like my lessons about recent efforts to end the genocidal mentality perpetuated by the representations of Native Americans on the Massachusetts state flag or the shift from Columbus Day to Indigenous Peoples' Day, my imperative as an educator is to provide my students with ways to consider how the past informs our ideas and attitudes about our society today. Oppressive regimes depend on keeping the truth from people in their efforts to legitimize and protect their power. This deception has been true in the past and is true today. Likewise, those who benefit—financially and otherwise—from exploitative institutions, practices, and policies are most often aggressive in their effort to promote ignorance under the guise that the lies they perpetuate are for our own good. For this reason, those of us who are committed to teaching what we learn—whether we're professional teachers or not—are engaged in one of the most noble human practices.

Does learning history prevent people, or nations, from making the same unethical and immoral decisions today? Sometimes it does, sometimes it doesn't. But whether or not we choose to use what we learn about the past to inform how we approach making our society and the world more humane and equitable *is on us*. As the late great poet June Jordan once said, "We are the ones we are waiting for."

STUDENTS, ARCHIVES, AND METAPHORS

Amy G. Richter

During the first meeting of our Clemente course, I call the students "archives." It is my cute way of encouraging them to be organized, take notes, save important emails, and keep track of assignments. It is also a pitch for the utility, richness, and joy of history (my discipline) and the humanities writ large.

Simply put, an archive refers to valuable records collected and organized by an individual or an organization. Archival documents can be seemingly impersonal (like a list of expenses) or intentionally intimate (like a love note on a napkin), but they all tell important parts of someone or something's story. Without archives, historians would have very little to work with in interpreting the past. Likewise, collecting and organizing assignments, emails, handouts, notes, and marginalia turns disparate courses, discussions, and readings into an *education* and empowers Clemente students to interpret course material for themselves.

Over time, the archive metaphor has stayed with me, deepening, challenging me to reflect on the power of what happens in our classrooms and beyond them. What does it really mean to recast people—especially Clemente students—as archives? Revisiting this question in a volume that is itself an archive of Clemente students' work feels particularly apt.

A good archive, like an engaged student, does more than collect, catalog, and preserve. Archivists make decisions about what documents have value. Sometimes this is risky because what we want to know changes over time. The archival challenge is to make decisions that build upon past priorities, reflect what is important in the present, and anticipate the questions of those who will come after us. For example, when I was in college, I did research in popular women's magazines from the nineteenth-century United States. My school's library had preserved the magazines in oversized bound volumes. Lucky me. Unfortunately, in many cases, the advertisements had been torn out to conserve space. I wanted to study the ads. I thought the ads mattered and could answer important questions about how women lived in the past. The archivists had not anticipated someone with my interests.

Inviting students to see themselves as archives is my invitation to anticipate their future selves—to both document and imagine the transformative possibilities rooted in meeting week after week. Throughout the course, we build a shared archive, reading the words of James Baldwin, Emmanuel Kant, Frederick Douglass, William Carlos Williams, and many others. We walk the galleries of the Worcester Art Museum and the stacks of the American Antiquarian Society (AAS), adding bits and pieces of these rich collections to our own. Together, we discover how our archives are like any other: living, dynamic institutions that at their very best want to be surprised, stretched, challenged, and reinterpreted by contact with others.

When we visit the AAS to explore primary documents hands-on, I see this "discovery" in action—both for myself and in the students. Many of the students don't know that Worcester is home to a world-class American history archive. Others have driven past the beautiful building without knowing what it houses. Still others understand it is some type of library—an "important" institution, but one with no connection to them. In preparation for our class, the archivists pull some of my favorite sources from their collection: a diary of a nineteenth-century domestic servant in New England, stereographs of Worcester, a Nellie Bly board game, paper dolls based on characters from *Uncle Tom's Cabin*, and hand-colored fashion plates from *Godey's Lady's Book*. These familiar items are joined by holdings I had never encountered in my own research: a collection of Puerto Rican newspapers dating from 1850; *The West African Record*; a nineteenth-century map of the Caribbean that includes Jamaica, the home of several students; *El Gato Bandido*, a children's book published in New York City in 1890 and targeting a new market of Spanish-language readers. In the course of our visit, the archive I thought I knew looks different as the archivists anticipated and welcomed our students, who in turn discovered their own histories preserved inside an impressive building they had not known was open to them.

Appropriately enough, the AAS has hosted our commencement ceremony the last few years. We walk into Antiquarian Hall with friends, family, and supporters feeling a sense of awe—and ownership. We understand as "readers" of the archive that it doesn't just serve us; we serve it, revealing the archive to itself by asking previously unanticipated questions. This is the symbiotic superpower we all share and celebrate in Clemente—each of us cataloging and surprising the archive, preserving, stretching, and challenging existing knowledge. The archivist builds the archive, the growing archive transforms the archivist, and the collection takes a new shape awaiting the readers who will see it with fresh eyes.

SANKOFA PEDAGOGY

TEACHING HISTORY IN BROCKTON CLEMENTE COURSE

Aminah Pilgrim

> As a classroom community, our capacity to generate excitement is deeply affected by our interest in one another, in hearing one another's voices, in recognizing one another's presence.
>
> —bell hooks, *Teaching to Transgress: Education as the Practice of Freedom*

The 2023 Brockton Clemente graduation was our most formal ceremony to date. Ten students completed the course, attending classes both virtually and in person. It was the first celebration held in person since the end of the COVID-19 quarantine period. Graduation took place at the Brockton Public Library, our home inside the city. Our program administrator decorated the hall beautifully and set up tables for guests and a photo installation for the graduates to take pictures of themselves wearing their caps and stoles. The majority Haitian immigrant cohort and their guests were treated to an elaborate meal catered by a Haitian chef. All were treated to a festively decorated cake that was adorned with the words "Congratulations Class of 2023!" The graduation speakers included the program codirectors, a student representative, a prominent pastor and community leader, the library director, and the city's mayor. Each highlighted the resiliency of the students who pursued their education during the end of quarantine, despite the traumas of the previous two years of the pandemic. It was clearly they, not the pomp and circumstance of the event, that was the most exceptional thing.

On the first day of my history course for each Brockton Clemente cohort, I introduce myself and my philosophy of teaching. I tell them that one objective of the course is to create community and that another objective is to create opportunities that foster personal growth. My wish is that the students will find themselves in the pages of the history texts, in the stories of ordinary people who made change. The principle of *Sankofa* guides the course. *Sankofa* is the name of a 1993 film on US slavery, written and directed by Ethiopian filmmaker Haile Gerima. We watch part of the historic film in class. The film launched a movement within Africana studies. The word (and its symbol) comes from the Twi language of the Akan people of Ghana, West Africa. Translated simply, it means "go back and fetch it" (or as I explain it to students, reclaim your past to power your future).

Armed with an understanding of *Sankofa*, we set forth on a journey to explore the multicultural and multilingual history of the United States as colearners, as coteachers, and as one community. In oral presentations, students are encouraged to make connections between their heritage country and US history. The results are transformative as each Clementino teaches and their peers demonstrate interest in the material. In the words of bell hooks, they experience "interest in one another, in hearing one another's voices, in recognizing one another's presence." Encouragement becomes contagious and momentum building. It is often a bit easier to generate excitement in a class with these conditions.

There are two *Sankofa* symbols. Each one is a powerful metaphor for the work of the Brockton Clemente history course. One depicts the two sides of a heart turning inward as if to face one another. I explain this as the two realms in which history exists—past and present—both necessary for a critical understanding of the subjects examined. The other symbol is of a bird with its head turned all the way back, looking back with an egg in its mouth—symbolizing hope and a future pregnant with possibilities. I tell students this sends a message that history examined can provide a blueprint for some of the pathways toward liberation and social justice.

As the course unfolds and we explore many of the topics in our textbook, Ronald Takaki's *A Different Mirror*, there is an expectation that we connect history with current events, and connect the local with the global (US history with the histories of the countries our diverse students hail from). Students are also nudged to write about or discuss their own current challenges and to look to the history of individuals or organizations that resolved to create lasting personal or cultural change. Starting the class in this way, with an African symbol, using a word from the Twi language, also signals to the class that we reject the "hegemony of English." This is a brave space in which they can bring their whole selves, recovering unknown parts of history and reframing their present and future selves.

In Brockton in particular, this makes sense. Massachusetts's first majority Black city, the residents include populations of African and Caribbean immigrants such as the Haitians in the class of 2023, among others (Cabo Verdean, Somalian, Angolan, Jamaican, Barbadian, etc.). The *Sankofa* concept and symbols resonate with their own cultural values, creating a familiar context, one that evokes joy and affirmation, one in which powerful learning can take place against a backdrop of acceptance. In their respective, individual *Sankofa* journeys, our students have overcome tremendous obstacles to arrive at the Clemente course—personal and collective traumas, loss of loved ones, addiction, being unhoused, and food insecurity, just to name a few. I remind them that the things they overcame are "receipts" for the strength they carry within them. They are invited to bring that strength and perspective to the study of history (and the other humanities classes in the program). In the classroom community, we can be present with one another and cocreate a healing, transformative experience within education.

CONTRIBUTOR BIOS

Summer Writing Class Students

CARMEN L. BELEN was born in 1987, in Jersey City, New Jersey, and later raised in Brockton, Massachusetts. Carmen, who is the mother of four amazing daughters, considers her faith, family, and mental health to be most important to her. If she isn't spending time with her friends and family, you can almost always find her trying to find more ways to better herself. An alumna of Clemente, Carmen is currently enrolled in an associate's degree program, with hopes of furthering her education and someday being able to teach literature.

JESSIE CHUKS was born and raised in the eastern part of Nigeria. She moved to Massachusetts a few years ago. She's a mother who is passionate about her Christian faith. She likes listening to music, reading inspiring stories, and writing. She expresses herself better in poems. God's arms is her go-to place.

LYNDA DOLIN was born and raised in Haiti in the beautiful city of Port-au-Prince before she moved to Boston, Massachusetts. Growing up, instead of playing with her dolls, she preferred to focus on her diary. Besides her family, Lynda is passionate about literature and romance novels, especially Harlequins. Lynda has a degree in marketing, and now she is studying communication. She is a Clemente Dorchester Alumni for 2022–23. Lynda's poem, titled "A Letter to My Son," is a narrative of the deep sorrow of a mother who is mourning her child.

JUDY GUSTAFSON is a devout Christian, a mother, a deaconess in her church, a writer, and a musician. Because she experienced homelessness firsthand, she has become a passionate advocate for the unhoused. Her life has definitely not turned out as she originally planned, and she is profoundly grateful. She lives in an apartment on the East Coast of Massachusetts with her cat, Shelby. When she is not spending time with her daughter, worshiping, tub-thumping, writing, or playing keyboards, she enjoys hanging out with her friends on the beach if at all possible.

BRIAN K. JOHNSON is a union member of SEIU 1199. I work at a large hospital in Boston Massachusetts. I'm a dad, brother, cousin, and so on. I was looking for a community during COVID and found the Clemente Course in the Humanities. The course gave me a place to be without being in person, along with new ideas and purpose. I can't say enough about the Clemente course for adult learning, and the programs they provide have also given me more interest in reading and writing.

GRI MARTINEZ SAEX moved to New York from the Dominican Republic decades ago. She considers Western Mass her second home, as it is where she has received many gifts from her roles as teacher, counselor, health care interpreter, mother, friend, and activist, and most importantly as a student of life. Gri loves where she is now, living and learning in the city of Springfield. Gri considers herself a budding artist thanks to the pandemic of 2020. Even though she studied Spanish literature and art in college, she concentrates on raising a family and serving her community. Today she writes poetry, creates clay pottery and sculptures, and paints and is a founding member and facilitator of Somos Semillas, a collective project directed by immigrants in the area. Gri was a recipient of the 2022 Marty Nathan Art and Activism grant, given by the Resilient Community Arts. She also attended the Clemente Course in the Humanities at Martin Luther King, Jr. Family Services, Springfield, Massachusetts 2022–23.

WILLIAM "BILL" MURPHY's story took him from Massachusetts to Viet Nam and back. Born in Dorchester, Bill's college years in Washington, DC, were rocked by the chaos of the city riots, antiwar demonstrations, assassinations of MLK and RFK, and the killing of students at Jackson State and Kent State Universities. As a draft-induced enlistee with his career plans in disarray, he joined the Army Security Agency and spent a year studying the Vietnamese language at Fort Bliss in El Paso, Texas. He served in Vietnam from April 1972 to February 1973, one month before the last serviceman left after the Paris Peace Treaty. "When I came back, I was floundering," says Bill. With the help of another Vietnam veteran, he embarked on a thirty-four-year career in federal law enforcement, investigating violent crime. Bill worked undercover in Boston's redlight district, the "combat zone," for a year following the murder of a Harvard University student. He helped solve the largest arson case in US history and the largest firearms trafficking case in the history of Massachusetts. He participated in the investigations of the 1996 Olympic Bombing, the Unabomber, the Amy Bishop University of Alabama mass shooting, Boston's Isabella Stewart Gardner Museum robbery—the largest art theft in world history—the Whitey Bulger organized crime group, and the Oklahoma City Bombing.

CHRISTO OWENS is a lifelong learner and student of the Clemente Course in the Humanities. Christo has an EdM in mental health counseling, focusing on youth and young adults. She is also an ordained minister and community advocate. Christo states her future goals include completion of her master's in divinity.

JESS RIVERA is a graduate of the Clemente Course in the Humanities in Holyoke, Massachusetts. Although the Constitution of the United States was established to protect the liberties of the American people, this author's lived experiences have led to their questioning, without hesitation, our true freedom. This individual is in the public eye and is currently advocating and researching sensitive topics and working to elevate oppressed people. You may reach this author at Iamhood007@outlook.com. Take action!

ALEXANDRA ROSA is a thirty-six-year-old devoted stepmom of two children and happily engaged to a chef. My roots are embedded in Puerto Rico, but I was born and raised in Springfield, Massachusetts. My journey began at the Clemente program when I registered to receive six college credits that would allow me to continue onto my next mission, college. My greatest achievement would be becoming a veterinarian and then running my very own animal shelter farm to rescue and place animals in happy healthy homes. I also would like to create programs for pet owners who can't afford pet ownership fees. My favorite place is when I'm writing poems. It makes the mind create magic. I love the energy I give throughout my poems and in the comments I receive from others. The mind is too valuable a thing to waste. Your dreams are more in reach than you think.

KELLY RUSSELL is a writer and poet from Boston, Massachusetts. She is a student of life and a constant work in progress. Too much time on her hands and her love for learning led her to find the Clemente course just prior to the start of the COVID-19 pandemic. Despite the challenges of education during that time, Kelly credits Clemente with reigniting her desire and drive to write after many years not doing so. She is a mother, partner, sister, and friend, and her writings cover a variety of topics that range from love, family, and personal struggles with identity to social justice, mental health, and incarceration. She is never one to shy away from a complex subject and writes through the lens of personal experience. Kelly lives in Boston with her partner, two children, and a menagerie of pets.

JAMIE LEE THRASHER is thirty-three years old, a mother of five and grandmother of one with one on the way. Writing is truly my passion, and the Clemente program has really opened up so many doors for me to achieve my goal. I have a story to tell, and my professors and classmates have encouraged me to continue on even after graduating. The Clemente program has truly changed my life for the better. I am truly grateful for everyone who has helped make my dreams become more of a reality.

MARIA M. WILSON-SEPULVEDA from Ponce, Puerto Rico, wife and mother, resides in the city of Brockton. She is an advocate for having information available in multiple languages, especially living in a city with a diverse community. She saw the need when her daughters began school and she found herself translating the information to ESL parents. She reached out to the Parent Information Center and worked with them to have the "backpack mail" available in the household's first language. She's also an advocate for ESL adult learners and ESL adult learners with learning disabilities. Many years ago, Maria put completing her college education on hold to help out her parents. In 2019, she decided that she needed to finish what she started. She registered and participated in the Clemente Brockton class of 2020 and then continued with the Bridge Program via Antioch University, Los Angeles, California, class of 2023. She's a firm believer that you're never too old to achieve your educational goals and that self-expression is beautiful in any language.

HAVA ZEJNULLAHU has been blessed with an amazing seven-year-old girl named Ella Hajzera. She resides in New Bedford but grew up in Brockton, Massachusetts, where her family had a furniture upholstery business for many years. She came upon Clemente in 2018 and never dreamed it would have opened so many educational doors, allowing her to meet so many people from all different walks of life and providing her the courage and confidence to pursue a degree. She thanks everyone involved at Clemente for everything they do to enrich the lives of others.

Independent Study Students

MURATZA AKBARI studied journalism in Kabul University, one of the best universities in Afghanistan. Currently, I live in Worcester, Massachusetts.

LOUISE BURRELL IS A community leader, a parent advocate who started the Good Street Project nonprofit to support the community, and the daughter of Henry and Mary Burrell.

JACQUELINE DOIRON is a free-spirited creator living in central Massachusetts. She is writing about her own life experiences to advocate for mental health services and to end the stigma associated with mental health and suicide.

DONNA EVANS is a lifelong learning advocate for BIPOC and Indigenous and senior populations.

DEBRA FRANCIS was born on Salandy Street on the island of Trinidad, Tobago in 1961. Her childhood home was filled with the members of her loving extended family which included ten brothers and sisters. Until her retirement in 2021, Debra served as a nurse at the Port of Spain Hospital. That same year, Debra received a green card through the efforts of her daughter, Alana Francis, and moved to Worcester. Interestingly, Debra was a role model for her daughter, Alana, who is also a nurse. However, Alana was a role model for Debra since Alana was the first in the family to graduate from Clemente Worcester. Debra followed in Alana's footsteps and received her diploma in 2023.

LARRY MADDEN currently works and lives in Worcester. His work includes army veteran, nurse, teacher, and writer always asking, Why?

THERESA QUINONES/BUCCICO is the author of *United We Stand through the Cries of an Opiate Orphan.* She is an aspiring motivational speaker. She currently serves as a recovery coach and community engagement specialist at

Everyday Miracles and psychiatric rehabilitation services coordinator for the community she grew up in, Worcester, Massachusetts.

DOREEN SAMUELS was born in Kingston, Jamaica. She is also a US citizen. She is known for advocating for the underserved and mostly for the homeless population and helping people access to resources in the Worcester community. She has a passion for helping anyone who needs her help. She is dedicated and committed to the people in her community. Her hope is that one day the homeless population will find a place to call home.

GEORGE THORNEY is lifelong learner and social activist specializing in promoting the rights and responsibilities of people with disabilities, those living with HIV and their families, spouses, and friends, older people, LGBTQ+ individuals, and immigrants.

Faculty

COREY DOLGON is a sociology professor at Stonehill College and serves as codirector of the Brockton Clemente program and the literature and culture professor. He was also the creator and instructor for this first summer writing course and book project. He is past president of the Society for the Study of Social Problems and the Association for Humanist Sociology. He has written dozens of articles and five books including two award-winning monographs: The *End of the Hamptons: Scenes from the Class Struggle in America's Paradise* (NYU Press) and *Kill It to Save It: An Autopsy of Capitalism's Triumph over Democracy* (Policy Press).

AMINAH FERNANDES PILGRIM teaches US History, Africana Studies, Women's Studies and Hip Hop Studies at area colleges. A scholar and community organizer, she is an advocate of teaching using civic engagement and has empowered many students to make a difference in this field. She is the Brockton Clemente Co-Director and History Professor. She is the founder of the HipHop Initiative (est. 2004), a critical hip hop studies collective. She is the co-founder of Poderoza: International Conference on Cabo Verdean Women, and the co-founder of Sabura Youth Program Inc. Lastly, she consults on matters of Equity and Social Justice in local school districts in the region.

OUSMANE POWER-GREENE is associate professor of history and director of Africana Studies at Clark University in Worcester, Massachusetts.

He completed his PhD in African American Studies at the University of Massachusetts-Amherst and his MFA in fiction at Columbia University. Over the course of his career, Professor Power-Greene's scholarship has been recognized with various fellowships, most notably the prestigious National Endowment for the Humanities–sponsored scholar-in-residency program at the Schomburg Center for Research in Black Culture in New York. Professor Power-Greene has been featured on podcasts and radio programs, such as *All Things Considered, CSPAN Book TV*, and NPR's history podcast *Throughline* for an episode on the legacy of Marcus Garvey's Back-to-Africa movement. As a Black studies scholar and historian, Professor Power-Greene's books include *Against Wind and Tide: African American Struggle against the Colonization Movement published*, by NYU Press in 2014, and *In Search of Liberty: African American Internationalism in the Nineteenth-Century Atlantic World*, which he coedited with Ronald A. Johnson and which was published by the University of Georgia Press in 2021. In addition to these scholarly works, Professor Power-Greene is also a novelist. His debut novel, *The Confessions of Matthew Strong*, was published by Other Press in October 2022 and is rooted in fifteen years of research and writing about the history and legacy of white supremacy.

AMY G. RICHTER is professor and chair of the History Department at Clark University and serves as the academic director and US history instructor for the Worcester Clemente Course in the Humanities. Her research and teaching focus on nineteenth- and twentieth-century American cultural history, with an emphasis on women's and urban history. She is the author of *Home on the Rails: Women, the Railroad, and the Rise of Public Domesticity* and *At Home in Nineteenth-Century America: A Documentary History*. Richter's teaching repertoire includes the courses Women in American History, Marriage and the Meanings of America, Gender and the American City, and American Consumer Culture.

ACKNOWLEDGMENTS

The Clemente Course in the Humanities is made possible in Massachusetts through support from Mass Humanities, the state affiliate of the National Endowment for the Humanities. Funding from Mass Cultural Council and private donors contributes to this support. Mass Humanities thanks the Clemente students, faculty, and our program partners: Brockton Public Library, Codman Square Health Center in Dorchester, the Care Center in Holyoke, PACE in New Bedford, Martin Luther King, Jr. Family Services in Springfield, the Worcester County Poetry Association, and the Worcester Art Museum.

Special thanks to Lester Spence, professor of political science at Johns Hopkins University, Martin Espada, professor of English at University of Massachusetts, Gina Ocasion, Clemente Course Coordinator for Mass Humanities, and Katia D. Ulysse, author and teacher, for their support of Clemente student writing.